OUR FATHERS BEFORE US

A novel by Martin Calvin

Published by

CORNELL DESIGN PUBLISHERS
P.O. Box 278
East Hanover, New Jersey 07936

Library of Congress Catalog Card Number: 83-71992

DEDICATION

This novel is a fictionalized work based on true characters. Any resemblance to any living person is pure coincidence and unintentional. It is lovingly dedicated to my grandfather, Hirsch Kapulkin, my uncle Nathan, my father Louis and to their wonderful wives.

It is especially dedicated to my beloved wife Etta.

I

****

Miami Beach, 8:00 A.M.

Every day he says the same thing--or he
does not say anything at all. If he says
something, then it's a shout. He
shouts, "No!" a single, huge report that
makes his chest hurt, that brings behind
it a wet, blinding cough. "No!" Kane
shouts to whatever kind of fancy car has
slowed along his walk and holds the curb
while its driver waits to hear the old
man's answer.

Sometimes there is none. Sometimes
there is just that harsh motion of the
head, the shaggy hair white, wild, flam-
ing in the early morning light, a grand
negation, abrupt and regal. And sometimes there is the lordly bellow, Kane's
colossal, thunderous "No!" the head not

even turning to regard the face of the well-meaning driver who feels compassion for the ancient Russian bolshevik Nathan Kane who would stubbornly persist in testing and taunting the oppressing heat and humidity of a Miami summer day.

"No!"

The old man with the enormous hulking frame does not walk alone. A black man in his mid thirties of equally imposing height and stature, of sufficient likeness to be Nathan Kane's shadow, walks by his side in synchronous motion. The contrast is stark and dramatic. Nathan Kane is garbed all in summer white while the man he mischievously calls Friday is dressed in black. Friday is Nathan Kane's manservant, bodyguard, and companion, who sees to his many needs, both real and imagined. He is possessed of the infinite patience to cater to the old man's excesses of humor and temper while providing for his physical welfare.

"No!"

It is a startling noise to hear. It is a statement of some ancient anger, furious with exuberant denial. It is an oath, a promise, an insult that hurtles through the scorched air, a frightful noise to suffer.

It is not a noise to be welcomed by

the condominium cliff-dwellers who stare
down from their pastel facades lining
this particular length of Collins Avenue.
For these are the tall buildings that
house retired Jews who have worked all
their lives in order to purchase a lease
on the peaceful outliving of their earthly
existence. The cost has been great,
and they want what they are paying for,
every last inch of sun-blushed, tranquil-
ized dying. What they do not want is
an old man's lunatic howling, a growl
hurled into the face of whichever quiet
citizen has this morning so thoughtfully
slowed his car and bent its path toward
the sidewalk to ask that mild, sweetly-
dispositioned question.

"Can I give you a lift, Mr. Kane?
It's so very hot and unfit for walking.
Your manservant is welcome too."

If the old man answers at all, then
it's a shout, and across his chest there
is a spasm of pain--and then the old man
heaves forward a little and coughs a lot.

But sometimes Kane just shakes his
head, the gesture rude, final, so utterly
expressive of contempt that were the in-
quiring driver blind from birth and an
imbecile to boot, he would nevertheless
know that a kind of monarch had spoken
and one was very lucky the reply had
stopped shy of the issuing of a sentence

of death. The large head delivers its
sharp retort, the great bushy crown of
silvered hair a brilliance in the awful
glare of light, and then the massive
body moves on, advancing itself as if its
parts were the honored components of
some ceremonial procession in high parade along the scalding sidewalk from
Harbor House South to Surfside Village.
The equally large black man, his face
drenched with beads of perspiration, follows in tandem close attendance.

It is August, and nobody walks.

The old Jews take to the comfort of
their air-conditioned Lincolns, or huddle
all day behind the candy-colored walls of
their condominiums. They have the good
sense to stay out of the public eye and
safe from the murderous vision of the
crazed Miami summer sun. Only Kane--
the bull, the union organizer brute, the
roughneck who got his millions bashing
strikebusters on the head so that he
could jump over the factory owner's gate
and then tear down his door and race
like an animal into his office to settle his
steaming hoof onto his soft, fat neck and
murmur nicely, "So, boychik, so tell me,
little boychik, tell your old pal Nat Kane
how come such a so-called respectable
business man can be such a sniveling,
capitalist twist of shit"--only this

madman Kane, in <u>August</u>, walks.

Behind the condominium walls that are blue and that are green and that are pink the citizens stir at the godawful sounds of Nathan Kane shouting.

"<u>No</u>!"

They hear him and they mutter: "In August yet. Only that <u>mushugineh</u> Kane. Listen to him. Rich but still a hooligan. A very rough diamond, that one, and also a very big moron. In August, the <u>alte</u> <u>Kocker</u> walks,--him and his football player <u>schvarzer</u> bodyguard.

The old Jews shake their heads. Necks swivel, a degree or so to this or that side, sometimes even to the wrong one.

"You hear?"

"Who couldn't hear?"

"And that's got millions. A regular fortune."

"A gangster. They say he killed people."

"He wouldn't need a gun. One peep from that mouth, an army would lie down and die."

"He thinks this is Rivington Street."

"He waked up my Harry."

"He could wake up the dead."

"You take away his millions, he's still a gangster."

"He's really a gangster?"

"Go know from a type like that."

"Don't sell him short. I heard he was once a very influential man. He hobnobbed with Presidents Roosevelt and Truman."

"You have to be joking!"

"No, I swear. He was a middle man in a lot of big deals and political hanky-panky."

"I'm impressed. I'll have to tell Harry."

"What's more he is writing a book!"

"I didn't know he could even read."

"He's not exactly writing it himself. He is spilling his guts, telling every-thing he knows--on tape."

"On tape?"

"On tape! You know--he's talking to a machine--a tape recorder. My nephew Irwin was in the Radio Shack store and heard him tell the salesman what he wanted. Kane made such a big todo--and with that monster schvarzer watch-ing every move--the salesman gave a sigh of relief when they finally left. He was afraid one wrong word and they'd tear down the place."

"And you said he's spilling his guts. Why? A thing like that could make a lot of people very angry. A man could get killed."

"You are so right. Why open old

wounds. It's water over the dam. Let bygones be bygones!"

"Maybe he wants to cleanse his soul before he dies? You know make peace with his maker."

"If that is it, he will need a ton of "Tide" and an ocean of water."

"If they come looking for him, I hear they will have a tough time finding him."

"How so? All they have to do is listen for a loud noise."

"Seriously, he has the penthouse apartment with no name in the mailbox--in fact no mailbox. He gets his mail at the post office and has an unlisted phone."

"If they want him they will find him. They have ways."

"It sounds like he is already hiding out."

"And what's with the big schvarzer? In a dark alley I wouldn't want to meet him! In fact I don't think I could see him. Who is he?"

"He used to be a tackle on a football team--the new York Giants I think--before he got hurt in a game. Name is Dearheart Hoskins. They sure have the most beautiful names, don't they? The old man calls him Friday--like in "Man Friday" from Robinson Crusoe."

"What else can he call him?

Dearheart? People would talk."

"I know what I would call him if I came face to face with him."

"What?"

"Mr. Hoskins, that's what!"

"My Harry's cousin Edna's in a Wednesday mah jong game, there's a very nice girl in it says she knows all about them, the Kanes. Newark and New York and Washington, D.C. He came to this country Kapulkin, and from Kapulkin he got Kane. He was once a what do you call it--a socialist? Then he got involved with the unions and from there to politics. Who knows--maybe even the mafia.

"And from this he got--millions?"

"He must have been doing something very right--or very wrong."

"So there's a wife?"

"Dead."

"Passed away?"

"My Harry's cousin Edna's Wednesday game says six months ago."

"From what? A wealthy woman like that?"

"The worst! What can I tell you?"

"Ohhh."

"And children? Does the old bastard have any other family?"

"One son, a genius professor out in California, from whom Kane gets no

<u>nachus</u> or nothing. They are estranged you might say. And a grandson Michael I think his name is--a lawyer in New York--who is the old man's entire life and joy."

Inside their pastel buildings the talk goes on and on. The retired Jews shake their heads and gossip. Nathan Kane is uniquely different and invites the curious to speculate and wonder. Meanwhile out in the street still another Lincoln is pulled over to the curb, a window dangerously lowered into the threat of the violent heat. The driver gapes in disbelief at the snarl that answers his courtesy.

"Mr. Kane, can I give you a lift? A man your age--be reasonable, hop in. Bring your manservant too. Look, he looks ready to collapse already."

They all do it. Every morning, always at eight, give or take a few minutes or maybe more, one of them wants to show off his fat automobile and his fat concern, and maybe, if you wouldn't mind listening, Mr. Kane, he'll tell you about his son, a wonderful young doctor, a regular magician, a nice Jewish boy, and then he would want to inquire as to what is truth and what is fiction with Nathan Kane. He would show pictures of his family and tell his stories and this would entitle him to know the old man's secrets. But Nathan Kane does not want to hear or see or share his thoughts with this Lincoln driver or any other. He still has his privacy and he means to keep it--at least until it all appears in a glossy hardcover book for Cronin & Keppler publishing company.

Does Kane answer? Does he open his mouth to bite the tails of their furry self-deceptions? Does he lower his wintry eyes into the whimpering arrogance of their sad, smug faces to roar certain truths about all the nice young doctors you'd never know were Jewish and about the slack-jawed imbecile in the picture, yes, that one, the boneless young fool with the sunglasses?

Why answer? What good would it do? So far as Kane is concerned, let them live with the petty lies that sustain them. The large truth of death will undo them soon enough--and, in the meanwhile, if Kane answers at all, it is just to shout "No!" to their big cars and their small satisfactions, "no" to everything that is easy and cheap and craven, and especially "no" to everything that is a lie.

They see the old man and his manservant making their way along Collins Avenue. They see them every morning at this hour. They see Kane's immense frame cutting a giant silhouette out of the fiery curtain the sun has draped before their eyes, and then they see the man's blazing eruption of hair, a flame in any light. The month is August and even at this hour the heat is already murder and the crazy goat is seventy-seven years old.

But the man is like iron. He gives nothing and he takes nothing. And if Kane answers at all, it's that same answer, and what it says is "no" to being old, "no" to being one of the boys, "no" to being fearful and to cowering together in their fright. It says "no" to being deceived, and "no" to being useless, and "no" to lying down so that death won't have to raise its fist and knock them down. It says "no" to being an old Jew whose idea of something worth paying good money for is the defrauding, cotton-candy indignity of Miami goddamn Beach.

Nochem Kapulkin will walk!

Nathan Kane almost says it aloud as he fastens his eyes once again on the lone palm tree that stands in the steaming distance ahead, and, the pain in his chest an agony, he renews his deliberate labor along the broiling concrete. His enormous black shadow trudges on after

him. But then, in just a few steps, the
liquids loosed in Kane's lungs stop him,
and he stands there, transformed into a
great woolly forest thing beating the red
air for breath and struggling to keep
himself from tilting headlong into the
earth. Friday watches the old man carefully, helpless to assist.

"Goddamn!" Kane howls aloud, when
the racking fit of spasms has passed and
he is restored to himself enough to try
the pavement again. He sees the tree,
that tall, solitary palm at the corner of
Collins and Harding, his beacon on these
walks from his apartment in Harbour
House South to his modest housekeeping
errands in Surfside Village. Kane rec-
kons his progress by that crazy tree,
queerly perpendicular for the kind of
growth it is, rising so thick and oddly
straight from the patch of meager soil
this side of the intersection. The shops
lie just beyond, the relief of their awnings, their cool interiors. But first
comes the tree, Kane's marker, his hand
reaching out to press briefly its smooth
bark and to receive its answering pressure, the sign that declares he has made
it once again, that once again Nathan
Kane has done what the rest of them
can't--and wouldn't even try.

No, not Nathan Kane, the old man

mutters to himself as he touches the tree and moves on, but Nochem Kapulkin, by God!

# # # #

New York, 8:00 A.M.
He cannot believe what he sees. He cannot believe this. He cannot allow himself to believe this.

A child is standing there, eyes wide, some sort of pink nylon, crib-size quilt clutched against her slender body, one corner of the thing sucked between her teeth. From where Michael lies, he could almost reach out and touch her if he wanted to. He did not want to. One arm is caught beneath the weight of a lissome female body--the other grips the top of the bed headboard, holding on desperately in shocked surprise--as if letting go would drop him into a abyss. The sleeping naked woman in his arms with the wildly cascading golden brown tresses is apparently the child's mother.

Something in his heart turns over and drops. Michael Kane closes his eyes and listens to it fall. He counts the seconds. But whatever it is, it will never hit bottom. He opens his eyes, certain that what he will see this time is just the regally furnished bedroom disclosing its elegance in the milky light, the expensive carpeting of sculptured yellow empty of real life, no little girl in thin nightgown and pink quilt standing there, one dainty foot over the other, eyes wide, appalled, staring.

She is there.

He wants to cry out "No!" He wants to call upon some fabulous magic and make her vanish. He wants to die.

He shuts his eyes again. He tries to do this subtly, as if to suggest that he is actually still sleeping, as if he is given to a manner of sleep in which the eyes open and close quite of their own accord, without relation to will or consciousness or vision. He decides there is nothing to do but to stay like this and let matters take their course. What will happen will happen. Because it has already happened. It is too late for anything else. The thing is done, and Michael Kane--who wanted more than anything else to be a father himself but was not, husband of someone who refused to bear him children--wants to die.

On the black screen that is lowered before Michael Kane's eyes, he sees what the child must see, the terrible spectacle revealed in the brightening dawn--two naked bodies woven into one gross formulation sprawled across the enormous circular bed, the discarded bed clothes revealing the combined nudity as some ungainly monster with four arms and four legs, startling and embarrassing with gaping revelation.

Oh my God, he thinks,--and then he hears "Oh, my God!" the words muttered, not screamed, and he feels the violent commotion of the mattress as the woman untangles herself from him and bounds from the bed.

Michael keeps his eyes shut tight, his heart aching for this woman whose frantic motion he hears, aching for the child whose voice is plaintive with shock and fright from the startling scene her wet saucer-like eyes had just witnessed.

"Mother, Mother, don't be mad, Mother! Mother, please, please, Mother!"

He hears the voice, a kind of sing-song cry, the pathetic volume of its beseeching dying quickly into silence under the carpet-muffled tread of the mother's heels moving out of the bedroom in rapid retreat.

Michael Kane knows that sound, the swishing of a mother's naked feet when she moves under the burden of a small child. He knows how the upper body is thrown back for balance against the child that is held cradled to the chest. Michael can imagine what he has not

seen--the woman coming off the bed in
one panicked motion, the body crouched,
the breasts suspended, the arms outstretched to sweep up the child and race
it away from a region of danger--broken
glass suddenly underfoot, a strange dog
turned nasty, something threatening
suddenly, some sudden jeopardy, havoc,
havoc! Michael knows these mother motions, the sweet particularities of ordinary maternity. But it is not through
his wife that he has learned them, for in
her Kane has witnessed none of the
abiding rhythms he holds to be rightly
common to all women, gestures in which
children find haven and husbands sol-
ace. He is willing to believe that it is
because of this that he is in this bed, a
man deprived of his proper bedroom pri-
vileges because of their schism--a dis-
agreement over whether or not to parent
children. Indeed, Michael Kane is willing to believe that the immeasureable
damage just done to this mother and
child is the sole fault of Mrs. Michael
Kane, the bitch whose cold indifference
sends him on these sexual errands.

He twists his large blond torso so
that he faces the bedroom door and can
watch the woman's entrance. His blue
eyes are open now, the eyelids still
sleep-swollen, but watchful and expec-

tant. The woman returns now, a hastily
donned negligee accentuating and cling-
ing to the relentless curves of her body,
her golden tresses a portrait frame for
the flawless features of her face. Her
expression is one of sheepish embarrassment. A smile lifts the corners of her
lovely mouth to reveal the perfect whiteness of her teeth.

"I am so sorry, Michael! Cindy has
never done that before. Her governess
fell asleep and forgot to lock the door."

The woman sits on the edge of the
bed and extends her arms to Michael,
inviting him to join her in a sitting
position. Michael covers his nakedness
with a corner of the sheet and moves
toward her.

"Come to think of it, Michael," she
goes on, "and you may consider this a
major compliment, I have never let anyone stay the night before."

Michael's expression is pleased but
yet one of puzzlement, her statement
having opened the door to more questions than it answered. The woman senses this and lightly caresses Michael's
cheek with her fingertips.

"Okay! Okay, sweet Michael. Because you are kind of special I'll give
you a very quick explanation. Cindy is
one of a twin. She has a brother

Barry. The two of them are a pleasant souvenir of an adolescent misadventure-- you know--older married man--couldn't divorce his wife--his reputation and you know all that other stuff."

"And how do you support yourself in such luxury and the kids--if you don't mind my asking--because I think you are kind of special too."

There is a bit of a pout. The con- versation has taken a highly personal path the woman has not yet intended to travel. To avoid the question or to re- spond other than honestly would termi- nate the relationship immediately, some- thing she is not willing to do. There was something about Michael that was lovingly familiar like the rekindling of an old flame--a comfortability she could not quite put her finger on.

"I'm a working girl!"

The statement hangs the words out plainly for Michael to see.

Michael's jaw drops, the meaning hav- ing a possible devastating connotation as they chase one another around in his brain: Does she mean "call" when she says "working?" Was there an implied price on all the wondrous things that had transpired this glorious night?

"No, silly, you can close your mouth now and stop looking like you are going to cry. I am not <u>that</u> kind of a working girl. I do special assignments for a business syndicate."

"What kind of assignments?"

"Oh--public relations, investigations, smoothing over bruised egos, finding out things--matters like that. I don't know why I am telling you all this. O.K.?"

"One more question. I have to know if you are working now."

"What do you mean, 'working now'?"

"You know, am <u>I</u> an assignment? Is there something you want from me?"

The gorgeous head is tilted back and shaken as her golden hair is fanned from side to side. A peal of laughter bursts from her upturned lips and fills the room with its frivolous mirth.

"The only thing I am after is your body, Sailor!"

Michael's head is clearing now. The events of an evening of cocktail partying followed by a night of glorious sex are now crystal clear to him. Her name is Denise something--or--other and they were introduced by Brad Hiller, a senior member of Michael Kane's law firm. The moment of meeting was magnetically electric and the feelings that followed even more so. For once for Michael the morning after looks as good or better than the night before.

They are swept into each other arms, their lips engaged in a passionate kiss. The negligee and sheet are quickly discarded as needless deterrants. Michael and Denise roll over and across the bed in a consummate embrace.

"What the hell is that?" they both cry out in unison to identify the annoying cause of their coitus interruptus. The persistent nagging of Michael's beeper is crying for attention from the nightstand.

"Oh, shit!" Michael screams. The joy of the glorious moment is obviously gone as he rises in his nakedness.

"Which phone can I use, Denise?"

Denise's expression is one of disbelief.

"Michael Kane, you son-of-a-bitch, do you mean to say you are going to leave me here on the threshold of my greatest orgasm to make a lousy phone call?"

"I am truly sorry, my lovely, but that is my hot line. The office only uses it for emergencies."

Denise's feigned anger now turns to convulsive laughter and Michael is drawn to join her as they contemplate the absurdity of their dilemma. When Denise can speak again, her laughter is reduced to a mischievous giggle.

"I though I was on your hot line,

Michael, but I can see I was disconnected."

"Don't go away! Keep warm! I'll be right back!"

Michael wraps the sheet around him again and quickly dials a number on the night-stand French telephone.

The voice of the communications patching operator responds.

"This is Michael Kane. Who is calling me?"

"Mr. Hiller, Mr. Kane, hold on please."

Clicks and buzzes.

"Michael?"

"Yes."

"This is Brad. Am I interrupting anything?"

"Yes, you are."

"Denise?"

"Yes."

"She is quite a girl, isn't she? I knew you two would make it together. Michael-er-uh-you aren't making it right now, are you?"

"Yes."

"You aren't going to say anything except 'yes'?"

"No."

"O.K. So you can't talk--but you can listen and this has to do with your grandfather. It's very important."

"Speak!"

"He has decided to write a book--
actually he's putting it all on tape--and
telling all he knows. You know--spill
his guts about a lot of things some
important people are going to be very
unhappy about."

"Oh, shit!"

"Michael, forget about Denise for a
moment and listen to what I am saying.
Some of those important people are our
clients! They want you to persuade him
to forget this foolishness--or else!"

"Or else?"

"They aren't saying exactly but the
inuendo is loud and clear. Nathan Kane
may get himself killed! And the firm
will lose some big clients."

"O.K., O.K., I hear you, Brad."

"They aren't fooling, Michael! They
are that scared of what he might say!"

"I will get down there right away and
take care of it. I promise you!"

He returns the porcelain phone to its
brass cradle and stands for a moment
engrossed in deep reflection.

"Hey!" the voice from the bed calls.
"Remember me?"

"Of course, Honey. Get ready!"

"Problems, Michael?"

"Nothing I can't handle."

Michael   discards   the   sheet   and

returns his nakedness to the bed. His body is there but his mind is still churning with the subject matter of the phone call.

"Well?" Denise asks, the question posed as much to refocus Michael's attention as anything else.

"Oh yes," says Michael, "now where were we?"

Michael's obvious fallen manhood in its own way is the answer to that question.

"Maybe we ought to start all over again?"

Before either one can indicate their willingness to commence foreplay, the voice of the French telephone speaks: two chimes and then silence.

"What's that?" asks Michael.

"A signal--that's my hot line. Now I have to make a phone call."

Michael sighs a sigh of resignation, the one that tells the story of something not meant to be.

As Denise steps boldly towards the phone, not bothering to don the negligee to shield her perfectly cantilevered breasts or meloned posterior from Michael's appreciative gaze, Michael plants a kiss on her cheek and reaches for his clothes.

"See you around, Baby."

Denise pauses, phone in hand-finger

poised to dial, a tear glistens at the corner of her eye prepared to roll down her cheek. Her voice is quiet, subdued, almost a whisper.

"Say this isn't a one-night stand, Michael. I will see you again?"

"You definitely will see me again!"

Los Angeles

It seemed to David that he was bounded on both sides, isolated by a trick of fate that dealt him a roughneck for a father and another for a son, persons of unhibited disposition. Perhaps David contrived his attitude to fit the way things had come to be. There was an essential animal difference that Michael and Nathan shared but had passed David by. Something in the genes, David thought. But nevertheless he found the characteristic difficult to cope with and impossible to be comfortable with.

At any rate that's the way it was between David and his father, and later between David and Michael. He called one Papa and the other Son, but he felt none of the connectedness those words are meant to be the emblem of. On the contrary, he felt an unbridgeable apartness from each of them.

David thought about the accumulated

feelings of his life as a son and thereafter as a father--and tried to analyze in
retrospect how things had come to be as
they were. Was he some kind of monster
to have drawn back from his own father
and then again from his son?

David remembers how Nathan would
come home from a day away, working at
God knows what. He scarcely knew as a
child what occupation sent his father
from the house on Smith Street so early
in the morning and then freed him to
return at all hours of the night. But
sometimes Nathan would come home early
enough to catch David still awake. And
even if his mother had already bathed
David and dressed him in his pajamas,
Nathan would beg to have his son bathe
with him again. There was this compul-
sive desire in Nathan to place himself
into some sort of intimate context with
David--always hugging him, always
touching him, always pursuing him as if
David were a pet of some kind, who, if
bathed in love would return it ten fold.
But he didn't--because he couldn't.

Mother would try to protect David.
She knew he didn't want it, that nakedness, the risk of seeing, of touching, of
being touched. If it were winter, she'd
make up one sort of alibi, and if it were
summer, another

"Boychik, boychik!" Nathan would be shouting as he plunged from the street into the house on Smith Street, reeking of smells that always struck David as foreign, or somehow brutally male and violent. He does not know what they were, garment-factory smells, he supposes, glues for use on fabrics, the acid pungence of cheap cloth, beer, the body fluids of the teeming humanity that seemed to be the element in which his father swam most powerfully. "Where's David? Where's the boy?" he'd shout after grappling with Mama, a greeting that looked to David like an assault.

He might be sitting in a chair against the wall, but David would feel as if he were hiding, trying to make himself smaller or more silent so that Nathan would somehow never spot him.

"Hey!" he'd yell when at last he'd rolled his eyes in the right direction, "there's the little darling! Come, sweetheart! Come, David darling! Come kiss this papa of yours the biggest kiss in New Jersey!"

David wouldn't move. He was paralyzed, maybe even terrified. He would try to hold himself so still that it would occur to Nathan that David was too fragile to be touched, that the merest fond-

ling might break him. But Nathan would
never be able to contain himself. For
long moments he'd gaze at David, waiting, the steam of utter devotion issuing
from his huge body. Nathan seemed to
want to utterly possess his son, consume
him, swallow him into his stomach.

"Go to your father," Mama would say.
"David, go give Papa a nice kiss." But
he could not move if his life depended
on it. And in fact, in his child's mind,
he thought it <u>did</u>. He wanted to
scream. David really thought that Nathan might suffocate him in some fit of
paternal passion. "David," Mama would
urge, coax, finally insist, "Go! All day
long your papa's been battling the world
just for you."

David stayed where he was, unable to
do as she said, simply unequipped to
move. He was like a woodland creature
who'd been trying to get safely from
here to there when its eyes are dis-
covered by the headlights of a passing
automobile. He was frozen in place,
converted to stone.

And eventually Nathan would come at
his son, hurtling down from his great
height, a bear, a giant, a great woolly
vitality that seethed like something on
fire.

"Ah, God, my son, my son!" he

would cry out like a man choking on love, and then he would sweep him up and crush him to his chest, squeezing the blood from his bones.

David's voice, it was so small in the same room with Nathan's. He would keep silent for fear of the shame. How could he say anything in reply--"Papa, hello" or "I love you, Papa"--when all he had to do it with was a voice so shamefully puny if lifted in answer to Nathan's throttling roar?

David would look around in dumb frenzy, terror seizing his brain like a fist. But always Mama would invent some plausible means of escape, and gently insert her shrewd sentence between him and the stormy giant who was his father.

"Later, Nathan darling, later. David is tired tonight." She would touch his back to reassure him. "You think this boy is made out of iron yet? Give him time to get strong like his papa."

In his own way, Nathan too would look around in a kind of dumb frenzy, stunned, his heart suspecting something he did not want to know.

"Sure," he'd say, and set David back down on his feet. "Better we don't take a chance, boychik?" And then he would ruffle David's hair and smile.

But David knew each time that his father had been mortally wounded. Yet, no, David was not sorry. In his mind-- then and now--he knew that if he wounded Nathan, it was only in self-defense.

At any rate, David sometimes thinks this is why he did not demand Anne terminate the pregnancy. He must have thought that the child would represent some sort of atonement for his distance from his father and from Michael. Not that he really thinks Anne would actually have done it, no matter how greatly David might have insisted. But he didn't. This was apparently what Anne had wanted all along--to have a child fathered by this man whom she so admired, her teacher, her professor. Was there love involved? As for Anne not in any usual boy-girl sense--but rather the fulfillment of a fantasy, an obsessive illusion born in precocious immaturity. For David it was the gracious acceptance of all the beauty that Anne had to offer. He was flattered though he could not really fathom. He was an idol accepting the adoration of a worshiper. How could he do otherwise?

Perhaps David was too stunned to offer resistance. Perhaps life--living things--has always left him too stunned to do other than go limp in the face of its onslaught. Books are safer things-- ideas held in the mind, organisms confined to the test tube, the memory of a Russian grandfather he never knew more attractive to him than the man himself might have been because of his sweet affection for his dark Talmudic studies. This David could comprehend, but not the extreme physicality and boisterous informality of his father and his son.

Miami Beach, 8:30 A.M.
Nathan Kane presses his hand to the lone palm as he passes it, and then, renewed, the old man strides briskly on into the shelter of the storefront awnings the Surfside merchants keep lowered day and night. Friday follows close behind, relieved to be rid of the relentless sun. Kane's immense body--tall and broad in the wide-waisted manner of certain large-boned, rangy men, men whose wrists are characteristically thick and whose forearms are invariably wrapped with veins that seem cut from rubber tubing--moves massively beneath the bleached awnings. Hatless and sockless, in white cotton trousers, white canvas deck shoes, white dress shirt rolled carelessly to just past the elbows, the old man is like a ghostly flag unfurling

itself along the quiet, empty sidewalk. You see his huge, stately approach along the path of shadow, and you sense something majestic and brooding about this silent colossus of a man, dark things seen, dark things done, things that have walled him up as with layers of mortar and stone.

His black counterpart, of equal outlandish size and proportion, looms like an ominous shadow guarding against any hint of threat or menacing gesture. Friday is clad in a black short sleeve football sweat shirt and cut off shorts. Perspiration has soaked through his clothes which cling to the massive muscles of his body.

Nathan Kane has changed nothing since Rose's death. He has continued to live with conditions that unnerved him in the course of her life, habits and circumstances that flowed from her wishes but which Kane has maintained in her absence. It is because these things suggest his dead wife's presence that Kane has kept matters intact. But it is a routine that he also despises if only because it is a routine. Custom, routine, fixed patterns of any stripe, these are things Kane has resisted all his life--for he regards them as limiting, death-laden, methods of conduct de-

signed for a country inhabited by lesser
men.   Old age is such a country, one
Kane understands to be the most powerful of all.   He loathes it and fears it and
wars against it at every turn.   And yet,
for Rose's sake, he was willing to make
perilous concessions to its relentless
dominion, chief among which was moving
to Miami Beach, to a section of it known
as Bal Harbour.   It was Rose's cancer,
her patient suffering, the woman's voice-
less petitioning, that at last convinced
Kane to give up the townhouse in
Georgetown and the apartment on upper
Fifth Avenue, to shut down the old
places and trim away the old alliances,
in order that he and Rose might take up
a life under siege in a pastel penthouse
atop a stucco vulgarism.   Condominium.
Kane hates the very word, its cheapjack
newness, its syllables, like the claim of
some fabulous science, hatched out of a
chemistry of synthetics.   He hears the
word and it makes him think of a new
wonder fabric reeking of plastics and
fresh minting.   It is a word that inclines
Kane to think of those other pomposities
that bully and yet entice the dying by
making them afraid-- mausoleum and
columbarium--words whose absurd sancti-
mony fill Kane with scornful laughter
and not with the respectful dread he

presumes their coinage was intended to inspire.

Condominium.

No!

Kane shivers with the thought that such a thing is now his home--all the old furniture gone, the dark heavy oak pieces, English and German, sold off, and in their place chairs and tables that look as if they were squirted from a can of Redi-Whip. But it was what Rose wanted, to get away, to try to leave her pain behind, to huddle with the rest that fled to Florida when death seemed about to catch them where they were.

Two blocks down he pauses at a newsstand to buy The New York Times and The Washington Post and The Wall Street Journal and The Daily Worker, the same assortment Kane still buys every morning even though it was only Rose that read the Times. Kane pays for the papers inside the sundries store that maintains the newsstand while Friday waits outside. When he sees Kane coming, the man at the cash register says, "One or two?"

Kane raises two fingers, and the clerk reaches in back of him to slip two packs of Camels off a stack and flip them onto the counter.

"Well, old mariner," the clerk says,

"you walk today?"

"I walked," Nathan Kane says, his voice a remarkably robust instrument for a man of his years.

"Must've been a dandy," the clerk says. "Not even nine o'clock yet, and it's up to ninety-eight. Muggy as all hell too."

"I have walked through worse," Kane says, stuffing the packs of cigarettes into his pocket and folding the newspapers under his arm.

"Yeah, well, there's always worse, I guess," the clerk says, ringing up the sale. "Can I offer you a glass of water?"

Kane shakes his head. "Maybe a shooter of cold gin," he says, "but water never. You ever look a fish in the face?"

The clerk smiles and shakes his head. "Nope," he says, "can't say I ever have."

"Take my word for it," Kane says, his deep voice stern, "it's enough to make a strong man cry. Stay away from water--that's my advice."

"Why, I do believe that's pretty sound advice, Mr. Kane. I'll take it."

"No charge," Kane says. "I have to go. I have to get back to my taping machine."

"How is the book coming, Mr. Kane?" The clerk feigns confidentiality and whispers "you think it will make the best seller list?"

The old man nudges the clerk's ribs with his elbow.

"It can't miss. All I have to do is live long to finish it. I'll save you an autographed copy." Kane laughs as he makes his way to the door.

It is a ritual between them, this exchange and the endless variations Kane and his interlocutor have worked upon it since Kane first came to Bal Harbour and started shopping in Surfside. It is true that he could do his shopping in his building's basement store, for his needs are not many or at all grand, and the little convenience store downstairs is certainly adequate to supply them. Or Kane could pick up a telephone and call his order into the village shops for easy delivery later in the day. But Kane prefers his walk because it is a labor--and Kane prefers Surfside because of the variety of tradespeople available to him in the village. Kane thrives on these plural contacts, the kibitzing with this one and that one, young people mainly, people who are just discovering the wonderful human pleasure of friendly fencing, the

quick and offhand play of the wits. In
turn, the huge approach of the old man
is always a welcome sight to the clerks
and cashiers who service Kane in the
fewness of his wants. They like to jest
with the old man, sparring with him in a
good-natured way, and, sometimes, for
their trouble, they find themselves
favored with a glorious anecdote from
Kane's years as a labor leader and a
consort of powerful men, of even presidents, or, better still, to hear tales of
his wild youth in a stetl in Russia, the
fierceness of his family's poverty, the
violent struggle and high adventure of
Kane's flight to America, his battling
triumphs against the small-time sweat-
shop operators enlarging to full-scale
warfare against the nation's industrial
giants. The old man is a splendid teller
of stories, a narrator with a fine ear for
the ironies of history and the follies of
men, himself included, himself first of
all. These young people admire this
gargantuan, solitary old man; they even
feel for Kane a sort of burnished affection, and a kind of pride in the fact
that he seeks them out and chooses to
pass the time of day with them.
They've never seen the old man with the
wife he used to have. They've never
seen him with anyone except his black

giant counterpart--who never speaks to
anyone but Kane unless spoken to. The
others of his age who make it into town,
they routinely travel in pairs or better
also,   doubtless   an   insurance   policy
they've signed up for on the principle of
safety in numbers. But the big one,
the one who favors garments of white,
him you never see with anyone save in
the loyal company of his dark companion.

Stories   circulate.   The   old   man's
striking appearance, the hammering icy
blue eyes, the burly arms and shoulders, the neck like a column of stone,
the crackling forest of white hair that
erupts in any light, these all contrive to
encourage a mythic account of Kane that
is, even so, less outlandish than is the
truth. Most have it that Nathan Kane is
a benevolent mobster, a Mafia chieftan in
retirement, a youthful strong arm spe-
cialist who survived the merciless years
of gang warfare to succeed to a position
of   ruthless   executive   power.   It   is
agreed that Kane could have you killed
by dialing a certain number. It is also
speculated   that   he   wouldn't   have   to
bother, that as old as the big man is,
he could break you in two with his bare
hands. No, they don't really believe the
tales Kane tells about life on the line as
a union organizer, about Sunday chats

with Truman and FDR. The young
people prefer the view of Kane as an
erstwhile hired killer, deeply philosophical, given to profound isolation, a hit
man who used to blow them away with a
wink and a nod because life didn't matter in the first place.

The truth is, on this particular
score, not so distant from the fiction--
for Nathan Kane has killed men, but not
for hire and not for gain, and never because he believed life did not matter. It
is also the truth that he did not have to
dial a certain number, but in fact accomplished the deeds, each time, three
times, with nothing more than the executive power of his own two hands. There
is also fantasy and speculation as to the
nature of the relationship between Nathan Kane and the aptly named Friday
who shadows him everywhere like a combination mother hen and FBI agent.
Some say that Friday's football career
was terminated when a head injury left
him with vertigo and occasional double
vision. Friday's father had been one of
Nathan Kane's faithful from the old union
days and the old man paid all the doctor
bills til he got well.

Less sympathetic tongue-waggers
project the theory that somehow the old
man bought his constant black companion

out of jail with a bail bond and is keeping him as a personal slave.

Still others say that Friday is the
watchdog of a mysterious syndicate that
has reason to keep the old man alive and
well forever.

There is, finally, more than a stroke
of accuracy to the notion of Nathan Kane
as a man occupying some terrible extreme of human isolation. But the larger
truth is that this is not a condition of
Kane's own choosing. He had a wife--
whom he loved greatly and lost not
easily--to death. He has a son--whom
he loves greatly and lost not easily--
to...?

Kane does not know to what. It is a
mystery, a riddle, that dumbfounds and
appalls him. It is an agony matched
only by Kane's anguished knowledge that
his greatest devotion was felt for a man
whom Nathan Kane thought felt nothing
for Kane in return. He was a man
named Hirsch. He was the man who
gave Nathan the name Nochem. He was
Nochem Kapulkin's, Nathan Kane's,
father.

It was a love that is now equalled
only by Kane's love for yet another man,
the fourth in a line that begins with
Hirsch Kapulkin, a teacher in a stetl
called Huika, not far from the city of

Moscow in Russia.

The man's name is Michael, this man that is fourth in a line of fathers and of sons that begins with that first giant of a man, a tranquil, inward, unloving teacher in a broken, blasted, ratsink called Horka.

Michael, the old man thinks, and the deeply tanned features of the seamed, leathery face seem suddenly livelier, as if the blood is astir behind them. "Ah, kiddo, kiddo," Kane murmurs to himself, as he moves up and down the aisles of the supermarket picking out first the items that need replacing, then taking some extra cans of salmon and an extra onion and several dozen, rather than the usual half a dozen, eggs. Then impulsively he adds a number of delicacies he normally would never buy.

As big as Kane is and as much of him as there is to keep alive, food is something Kane uses only insofar as the need is strictly announced inside him. Yet he relishes the least morsel put before him, the legacy of a youth that was never very far from the threat of absolute starvation. For himself, a can of salmon and an onion to chop into it, and the egg to form the mixture into a pattie, is ample for the day's nutrition, so long as there's cracker to nibble, a bit of crisp matzoh, some tea, some gin or bourbon or vodka. Friday has learned to eat and thrive on whatever the old man eats. But today Kane buys many additional rations--because sometime soon he knows that, his grandson, Michael will be coming! And maybe even by some miracle, Michael's father, Nathan's son, David, too!

"Ah, Michael, kiddo, oh, kiddo," the old man croons to himself as he wheels the shopping cart to the checker and stands waiting for the young man to run up the few items and bag them.

"You'll do a decrepit old thing a favor, sonny, yes? You'll break your heart and give him a nice large bag, bigger than he really needs, and then a separate bag so he's got a place to deposit these newspapers?"

"Sorry, sir," the boy says, grinning impishly, "this here store's management got a rule on that. Extra bags only if you're carrying four copies of The Miami Herald."

Kane throws up his hands in dismay.

"My God, what is this, The Miami Herald? That's a newspaper?"

"It's a fact," the boy says, a bit off his stride with Kane to see the old man buying so much more than his usual purchases.

"So who reads this newspaper?" Kane says. "Real people? American citizens like you and me?"

"It's a fact," the boy says, punching in the tax and ringing up change from the fifty dollar bill Kane hands him.

"My God," Kane says, blowing out his cheeks and dripping his shoulders in a show of total surrender. "But to tell you the truth," Kane says, brightening, "at my age, sonny boy, it's no fun to face facts, whereas at your age each new one is a regular adventure. So big bag, please, or I'll piss on your cash register."

The checker shakes his head, noiselessly whistling. He yanks two large bags from under the counter, fits one inside the other, and puts in Kane's grocery items. He takes out a third bag.

"Give them here," he says, and takes the newspapers from Kane. He wedges them carefully into the third bag. "Can you lift them both, old man? Or shall I call Friday over to carry them for you?"

Kane snorts. He'd like to hug this fresh-faced, crisp young item, this clean American boy over-running with healthy animal spirits. Nathan Kane would like to pick the fellow up and just hug him hard, so moved he is by the great affection he has for the bumptious zest of the young. But it is the two big bags Kane picks up instead, not hugging them to his chest but holding them off to the side under each arm, a small display of not much strength, but a critically prideful maneuver in these circumstances.

"You got company coming, Mr. Kane?" the boy calls when Kane stops at the empty checker station near the exit to set down his groceries for Friday to take and light up his first cigarette of the day.

"Grandson," Kane calls back, smiling like crazy despite himself. "And maybe if I play my cards right--maybe even my son."

"Hey, that's swell," the boy calls, a little surprised. Somehow it's hard for him to connect this giant, white-draped figure with such unremarkable events as marriage and paternity. "But if they are anything like you, they will really be something special."

A wave of concern passes over Kane's face, but the expression is fleeting.

"Something special? Like me?" Kane calls to the checker. "Hell they are my family--my only family."

His voice drifts off as he walks toward the waiting Friday.

"There's no one else left now that Rose is gone."

Kane is at once stunned by what he has said. He had meant for it to come out some sort of quip, some kind of smart-aleck reply built on the motif in his opponent's thrust. He'd given the thing no thought at all. Instead, he just rolled with the rhythm, opening his mouth for an utterance he expected cadence to improvise cleverly on his behalf if he only kept his mouth going. But what came out wasn't clever at all--far from it. It was dumb or it was meaningful--for it seemed to be saying something Kane doesn't exactly understand but something potentially confessional, temptingly revelatory, as if in his race to achieve a kibitzing reply, any kibitzing reply, his tongue's foolish rush yanked loose a chunk of strange truth. But no, it is ridiculous to make too much of this, a piece of clumsy speech, a mere rogue remark--it is nothing, not anything of any consequence at all. Words, just words, and with this Kane throws off the mood the thought has dumped him in. He waves goodbye to the young checker, and follows Friday through the automatic door.

The heat is already a thousand times worse, and worse than the heat is the

cloud of wet molecules suffusing the
scorching air, a washrag thrown in the
face. The old man almost staggers from
the shock of so rapid an exit out of per-
fumed, air-cooled space into the rotting
humors of the street. The walkways are
still virtually empty of traffic, and only
a few cars cruise sluggishly by, but it
is already as if the sweat of every citizen has been collected and set out to
boil on the fire.

Nathan and Friday lean into the
thickening heat toward Bal Harbour and
the Harbor House apartments.

The old man touches the solitary palm
as he passes it, crosses Harding, and
travels slowly on into the terrible fevers
of the day. But the walk home is not so
bad--for his mind and heart are far
away from the brutal business of getting
from here to there through the soupy
weight of the August air.

"You O.K., Friday?" Nathan Kane
asks as he pauses for a moment and
glances back. "I would hate to have to
carry you the rest of the way."

The rows of white teeth flash in a
brief smile.

"I'm just fine, Mr. Kane. You all
right?"

"I'll make it," the old man says. "I
always make it."

Kane does not hear the car at first--
but when he does, he does not turn.
He hears the engine slow. He hears the
insect buzz of the hot tires on the hot
asphalt. He does not turn around. He
can sense the slowing of the car, its
steady motion in pace behind him, the
gradual veering toward the curb. He
waits to hear the voice calling through
the lowered window, a plaintive whine or
a bombastic command:

"Hey, Mr. Kane. I beg your pardon,
but it's murder out there. Maybe you
should hop in and I'll give you a lift
back. What do you say, Mr. Kane?
Can I give you a ride?"

But that is not what Kane hears, nor
does he hear: "Kane! Be reasonable,
for God's sake! Get in and let me take
you back! You'll drop dead from schlep-
ping yourself in this kind of weather!
You hear me, Kane? So give me a civil
answer!"

What Kane hears is just the wheels
slowly turning, the car cruising along
the curb very close behind him. He
does not turn around. But Friday does.
He sees the sun's rays reflecting from
the blue-black sheen of the gun barrel
as it pokes its ugly nose through the
half opened window. Friday leaps as he
has been trained to do when the oppos-

ing full back is thundering his way--
threatening to invade his space--the
little corner of the world that he will
defend with his very life. Now Nathan
Kane is his responsibility. Friday drops
the packages and vaults through the
torrid air, in one fell swoop bringing
Nathan Kane to the pavement cradled
under the black man's massive body.
Shots rocket out from the car--one-two-
three-four!

The automobile engine races with a
roar, and the car screeches away down
the street, its screaming tires crying out
like banshee ghosts.

The two Goliaths lie there black on
white in disarray like some kind of car-
nival pretzel, the groceries and newspapers somehow still standing self-
contained in their respective bags.

"You all right, Mr. Kane? Are you
hit, Mr. Kane?" Friday's voice is anxious and angry.

"I will be--just as soon as you get
your ugly body off my back. I told you
I wasn't going to carry you home."

With this Nathan Kane rolls over to a
sitting position. He is roaring with
laughter as he slaps the steamy sidewalk
to emphasize his glee. The mystified
Friday brushes himself off as he
scrambles to his feet.

"You are a strange man, Mr. Kane, just like they all say. You almost get yourself killed and you sit there and laugh like a lunatic."

The old man pauses in his laughter and winks at Friday who is helping the old man regain his feet.

"Don't you see? I have their attention! They finally know about my book and my tapes."

"What is so great about that?" Asks the perplexed Friday. "They could have killed you. They could have killed both of us."

Again the old man winks.

"Exactly, my friend, they could have killed us if they wanted to. It was a warning. They will wait to see if I get their message."

The old man stiffens his back, motions Friday to follow and moves on, his towering frame heaving into the maddened heat. Again the sound of an automobile slowing is heard but instead of gunfire, a frenzied succession of six horn bursts, like six stubby nails hammered rapidly into the smooth grain of the morning.

Kane does not turn to look. But now he shakes his head, a signal of furious refusal. Friday readies himself but sees it is a police patrol car.

There is instantly the angry snarl of rubber jerked against pavement, and then, out of the side of his eye, Kane sees the sudden rush of the patrol car cutting in ahead of him, slamming over the curb, and flaring to an ugly halt, the front wheels black and seething on the sidewalk.

"Hold it right there!" the man in uniform is saying as he shoulders out the passenger door, his big, round, puffy face red with rage, sweat mapping dark discs through the tight, contoured shirt, the heavy firearm slung so low from the gun-belt that the butt wobbles clownishly.

Kane cannot believe this. He just stands there, waiting to see what will happen next, his attention fixed on the dense black sideburns, the florid face, the small hooded eyes. Friday steps back trying to be as unobtrusive as a man his size can be. He wants no part of this.

The man in uniform plants himself squarely between Kane and the car, arms folded, both hands balled beneath the biceps.

"You deaf?" the man says. "How many times do I have to horn you down before you got the brains enough to stop?"

"I didn't see you," Kane says mildly. "I heard you, but I thought it was somebody trying to give me a ride. People are always trying to give me a ride, yes? I don't like it."

The man is standing still, but he seems to be hurtling at Kane. Is it a trick of the heat, the vapors moving?

"Don't hand me that crazy shit. You and your nigger having target practice disturbing the peace? Now you get your goddamn identification out where I can see it and you do it fast, mister."

"What?" Kane says. "What is this?" Kane says. Suddenly it is not easy standing here this way. Suddenly something is very wrong. The cement beneath Kane's feet seems to be curving, bending up and then twisting off to one side.

"You heard me," the man in uniform says. "Now I'm not going to fuck with you, mister. You do as I say and you do it now."

He wants to lie down on the sidewalk and maybe disappear between the cracks. He wants to get down low somewhere because up here everything is beginning to swerve off into queer meltings, things solid and stable going soft and runny. The old man tries to steady himself, but something in his head or in head or in his belly, some switch that makes things work right, won't click on.

Kane stares hard at the small, hooded eyes, and it is then that he notices the deep lateral cleft carved into the fattish chin. It reminds him of something, this abrupt tuck in the brutal face. It is a fold of flesh set into a face not unlike some other face. But what face? Kane cannot place it. Someone recent? Someone long ago?

"I'm not telling you again, mister! You get that goddamn ID out here, or, by God, old as you are, I'll crack you one."

It is the cleft in that chin that Kane is looking at when he answers, his voice level, his words strangely precise and calm.

"I am old, officer. I see you noticed. Perhaps you also noticed I am big, yes?"

"What?" the man in uniform says. "I hear you right? You say what? Listen up, motherfucker, I've had me some crazy yids on this patrol, but you fucking take the fucking cake! Big you say? Now you wouldn't be threatening a peace officer, would you? You going to sic your nigger on me--or are the two of you going to gang up on me? Where's the fucking gun?"

Kane speaks quietly. He just wants this heat apparition to go away--disappear to whence it came.

"There isn't any--as you say--fucking gun. Someone shot at us from a speeding car."

The officer spits into the dust and stamps his foot as if to emphasize his impatience.

"Now why the fuck would anyone want to kill an old bastard like you and his Ninny--and how could they miss two targets like you? If they shot at you, why aren't you dead?" The officer comes forward a step, but then he takes two steps to the rear and lowers his arms. "All right," he says, "I've had all the Jew and Nigger shit I'm going to take today. Now you are alleged disturbers of the peace fleeing from the scene of an alleged assault. And I am a law officer in fucking pursuit. Now I'm asking you nice and I'm asking you for the last time, identify yourself to my satisfaction."

Kane starts to put his hand behind him to remove his wallet. The officer's fingers move to grasp the handle of his awesome weapon. "If that hand comes out with a gun in it I will blow you away." The old man checks the motion and instead reaches his hand into a side pocket and leaves it there.

"No," he says, "I don't think so. I don't think I'm going to do what you want. You understand? I refuse."

The man in uniform looks bewildered for a moment. He shifts his weight. He props the heel of his hand on the butt of the low-slung pistol. He stares at Kane. When the man speaks, the voice is almost a whisper, a hoarse croak full of true fury. "Now I'm going to tell you something, mister. It's just you and me and that fuckin' nigger out here, and I'm going to fill you in on the whole fucking score. I don't like you people. I don't know which of you I hate more. Fact is, your kind make me fucking puke. So it don't matter diddly shit to me that you're an old bastard, and it don't matter diddly shit that you may be telling me the truth. All that matters is I'm just tickled to fucking death I got some kike bastard and a nigger with their tits in the wringer caught creating a disturbance and..."

But the man in uniform does not finish. He stops himself in mid-sentence to yank his head around to the approach of another car, a big brown Lincoln that has pulled over to the curb. A squat man is getting out, his short legs carrying him quickly up onto the sidewalk.

It is Goldmesser, a neighbor of the old man from Bal Harbour.

"Mr. Kane," he says, and nods. "Officer."

The policeman pivots slightly, and takes his hand off the gun butt. But he seems uncertain what to do with his arms.

"Officer Foley? Am I right? You remember me? Goldmesser?"

The man in uniform looks back at Kane. It is an odd look--almost wounded.

"There's trouble here?" Goldmesser says. "Mr. Kane, you don't feel so well? Officer Foley is coming to give assistance?"

Neither Kane nor the man in uniform speaks. Goldmesser looks coolly from face to face.

Kane can barely keep to his feet any more. He rocks from side to side to keep from falling, his body like a sack of cinder blocks now.

Goldmesser smiles. He raises his hands as if waiting for someone to fit on gloves. He says, "Officer Foley, we'll let the old gentleman here sit in my car while you and I have a chat. Is this agreeable?"

The man in uniform seems stunned. His assent is the merest inclination of the head, a tiny lowering of the swollen jaws.

"Mr. Kane?" the short, squat man says, motioning with his eyes. "My car?"

Kane stands where he is. He does not look at the little man when he replies.

"I walk," Nathan Kane says.

Goldmesser smiles pleasantly, a man who will indulge any madness. He shrugs his shoulders and then reaches out his fingers to the arm of the man in uniform. Kane can hear what the little man says. He hears, "Come, Officer Foley, we'll have a little talk."

It is a sound Kane despises, that peculiar tone that is half-humoring, half-wheedling, and wholly conciliatory. It is the voice of reasonableness, of getting by, of making do, a propitiating of the angry gods and of meanwhile getting the better of them.

Kane looks once before he starts around the smouldering hood of the patrol car and continues on toward home. Friday, his face a mass of raging fury, falls in step behind him. The old man sees the man in uniform and the small man strolling very slowly up the sidewalk, in the other direction, the little man with one hand tentatively working at the elbow of the big man, the other hand reaching back to remove his wallet.

Kane fixes his eyes on the distance left to go, and he walks, his legs so numb they're cold. He hates himself for what he thinks--that he loathes his savior no less than his antagonist. But he is willing to recognize the truth of what is in him. Still, the thought is not with Kane long--for after a few steps it is pushed aside by the vision of that trench-like crease in the lumpish chin, the profoundly vivid but elusive reference to a tsarist brute long forgot but now remembered. Yet even this piece of business does not stay with Kane for very long. Two steps, five steps, what does it matter when it is not enough steps to get him the distance he must go? But the old man is not walking when it happens. The old man has stopped himself to see where his legs have gone. When he looks up again to correct his course into the radiance ahead, the light pouring from the sun turns to black water, and the earth rushes up to carry Kane down.

# # # #

New York, 9:30 A.M.
Michael's mind is a maelstrom torn by

divergent winds pulling him at once in all directions. There are decisions he must make that cry out in their urgency. He wants to settle his marital matters once and for all. And he hates to leave Denise. The hauntingly beautiful woman who hints of strange, mysterious secrets draws him to her with an irresistible force. And now the safety of his beloved grandfather, Nathan, is at stake and he knows that all else must wait.

The taxi is just making its approach. It is heading for the ramp leading up to the roadway that carries Queens traffic over the bridge into Manhattan when Kane leans forward and calls to the driver, "Hey, pal--let's turn around and take it back to LaGuardia."

"The hell you say," the driver says.

"You heard me," Michael Kane says, sitting back in his seat. "LaGuardia."

The driver pulls over to the side and stops.

"You say LaGuardia?"

"Right. You want me to spell it?"

"Mac, we were five minutes from La-Guardia when you got in fifteen minutes ago."

"Listen," Kane says menacingly, leaning forward again, resting his big hand on the back of the front seat, "I'm not looking for any geography lesson, and I don't need any argument, either. Let's move it, okay? I got a plane to catch."

"He's got a plane to catch," the driver mutters, and pulls out into an illegal U-turn. The Saturday morning traffic is mild, but even so this kind of maneuver so close to the bridge ramp is complicated, and the driver shakes his head and silently curses as he struggles to get the car started back in the other direction.

It's not yet ten o'clock when the taxi leaves Kane off at the Eastern Terminal. Kane checks the departure flights displayed on the schedule board. Nothing for several hours. He goes quickly to the Delta terminal to see what they have. He sees an eleven o'clock departure listed, a flight that lands at Fort Lauderdale, which actually puts him closer to Bal Harbour than the Miami airport does.

He looks around for a flight agent and spots one right behind him.

"You got a seat on Flight 84?"

"A seat?" the agent says, smiling. "This time of year? How about half a plane?"

"Swell," Kane says, and glances at his watch.

He goes to the nearest phonebooth and places a call to Nathan. The thought that consumes him is the possibility of the old man's life being in danger.

He thinks "What the hell is Nat up to? After all these years he decides to write an expose? It's out of character! Nathan Kane wouldn't squeal on anybody if his life depended on it. Hey--maybe that's it--maybe somehow--some way--he feels his life--what's left of it--does depend on it--or may be the old guy has finally gone senile. It's possible. Nah! It's impossible! He wouldn't tackle such a project if he were senile!"

Round and round the thoughts go in Michael's head, bouncing off one another trying to find answers to riddles that have no logical base in fact.

"That number is not answering," the operator says.

"Let it ring some more," Kane says. "Maybe he's sleeping. Sometimes it takes him a long time to get to the phone. He's old."

"I'll keep trying, sir," the operator says.

Kane fires up a cigarette and waits, turning the heavy martial lighter slowly in his hand as he works out a picture of Nat just coming in the door, or Nat just waking up from a little doze, or Nat getting out of the shower in a hurry to catch the phone before it stops ringing.

Hey, old man, come on, Michael
thinks as he smokes and waits and wonders how much longer the operator will
keep this up. He must be out because
Friday would have certainly answered by
now.

"I'm sorry, sir," the operator says.
"I can try that again for you in fifteen
minutes if you want."

"Skip it," Kane says. "Thanks."

Michael continues to sit for a moment
in the phonebooth, receiver in hand and
finger poised to dial his wife. He really
ought to tell her he was leaving town--
ah! she would only give him an argument. Nah! He thought Elaine Kane
wouldn't and couldn't care less whether
Michael Kane caught a slow boat to China
or Timbuktu. She's got her career and
her tennis and her social snob friends.
What else does she need? "Fuck her,"
he thought, he'll explain it all when he
gets back.

He hangs up and goes to stand in
line at the Delta counter.

He has a more pleasant thought that
brings a sneaky smile to his handsome
face: Denise! What a girl! Wow!

He takes out his wallet to see how
much cash he has-and finds enough for
a cab from Ft. Lauderdale down to Bal

Harbour, with maybe enough extra to buy a toothbrush and toothpaste and a disposable razor and shaving cream before he gets on the plane. The credit cards will take care of the rest-besides Nat won't let him put his hand in his pocket for a nickel anyway. It will be good to get away from Elaine, the turbulence of their marriage and their pending divorce. Every time Michael thinks about Elaine he feels as if someone's reached inside him with a big spoon and scooped out his guts. It makes one wide, swift sweep, scrapes everything clean, and when it's yanked out, it's brimming with vitals, and there's nothing left inside him except a bellowing hollowness and a terrible silent crying and the mute tears that weep for a love gone sour. Maybe it's just as well they hadn't had any kids to get in the middle of this.

He stands in line, waiting. He looks at the overhead clock and then he checks his watch and moves the minute hand from the three to just after the four. He shifts his weight from foot to foot and then he leans out of line to see how many are still ahead of him. It is then that Kane first sees the woman.

It makes Kane catch his breath to see her. The sight of her, just that glimpse, sets a nerve deep within him into high throttle, a tumultuous commotion that is as the stirring of a profound instinct, some basic human need--the getting of food, self-defense--called forth into violent assertion. She is a perfect female specimen, a thing perfectly formed, perfectly adorned in limb and feature, a kind of textbook rendering that might be exhibited under the title WOMAN.

But it is not this that makes Kane catch his breath and tremble. No, it is something else. There is something else--at once hauntingly familiar and yet obsessively unique. He doesn't see her face yet. Her hair is bound up in some sort of exotic turban so as not to reveal its character or color. Michael Kane grins with embarrassment and surprise-- he almost laughs. He steps back in line and then steps out again, this time to really look hard.

She stands three places ahead of him, her face is turned away from him as she focuses her attention off to a side. Kane looks and sees two small children in pert sun-suits and gleaming red sandals, a dark-haired boy and a dark-haired girl. They stand idly in front of a row of chairs holding hands. Kane looks back to the woman. Now he can

see her deftly sculptured face in profile,
the highset cheekbone prominent on this
side of the face, the dark brown eye
well wide of the long patrician nose, the
bold jawbone running sharply back to
the full throat, the little pleat etched
from smiling curved crisply into the olive
skin to form a bracket around the vertex
of the bowed letter V seen in Kane's
half-view of her lips. My God, it is
Denise! Her name almost shouts itself
out of his throat. But he catches himself in time and holds back. Surprise!
Surprise! What is she doing here? Stupid question! Obviously she is taking a
plane to Miami with her two children.
Michael's mind circles back to try to
remember if she had made mention of any
such plans. Oh, yes! Denise had said
she had a dentist appointment this morn-
ing--which would tie her up. What happened to change her plans? The phone
call of course! A working assignment!
Michael decides to observe things for the
moment. She wears blue jeans, evenly
faded and clearly of some boutique de-
signer make, for the fit is too con-
sciously expressive of the buttocks and
legs beneath them to have been the for-
tuitous work of some machine. It is also
obvious that if she wears a brassiere, it
too must be the product of a costly piece

of ingenuity, for the desired effect that she wears none is what is intended, and in this woman's case it is, Michael surmises, an effect worth every nickel of the tidy sum it must have cost. He is willing to take the same view of the slightly too small white cotton T-shirt she wears, a skimpiness that is very much in the current fashion and surely must have originated in Paris or Rome. Certainly the same must be said of her shoes, also, like the children's, sandals, and also, like the children's, gleaming red--but unlike theirs, the few strips of patent leather would likely be very expensive.

Kane gazes at Denise. She does not yet notice him, obviously one of those fortunate females well-accustomed to being stared at by men. He studies every square inch of what is communicated by the choices that have gone into the selection of her attire, the wonderfully floppy, saddle-leather handbag, more a carry-all really, that is slung nonchalantly over one shoulder, the long strap artfully hooked from the tips of two fingers drawn back to just above the right breast, the weight of her body accordingly situated so that one hip is thrust rakishly to the side, a sort of oh-God-they-dare-to-keep-me-waiting statement for the information of anyone who cares to look.

Many do. Kane sees that he is not the only one whose attention is seized by the spectacle of this woman. He can see that she is the kind of woman who is used to compelling notice and who enjoys it. It makes him think of his wife Elaine, this effort to attract the glances of people in public places. Except in Elaine's case, success succeeds in annoying her once she had it, and Michael can't even count the times she has turned peevishly to him to say, "That man there, Michael! He's absolutely staring at me. It's outrageous, it's absolutely infamous. If you're any kind of a man, you'll make him stop!"

What is she doing here? Kane thinks. Is anyone else with her? Kane looks around to see--but there is no likely candidate. What does Denise really do to finance her taste for hundred-dollar blue jeans and eighty-dollar T-shirts.

When Kane looks back to the woman, she has moved up in line to the counter. He strains to hear what she is saying-- to determine for certainty the destination for which she is purchasing tickets.

He hears nothing. He sees only her teeth flashing as she every so often, while in the midst of a sentence, turns to glance off to her children, and then, more quickly than Kane would like, the woman is gone, having conducted her business at the counter, collected her two children, and, walking between them as she holds their hands and leads them away, moves off toward the security check and the departure gates.

"May I help you, sir?" Kane hears when he wakes from his reverie to find himself first in line and facing the practiced smile of the salesgirl in front of him.

"Yeah, sure--you bet," Kane says, digging in his wallet for his American Express card. "A coach seat on 84 to Miami."

"That flight goes into Fort Lauderdale, sir."

"Right," Kane says. "Sorry. That's swell."

"Return space?"

"No thanks."

"One moment, please," the girl says, clicking her fingernails across the keyboard of her computer terminal. "Smoking or non-smoking?"

"Uh, smoking," Kane says, his mind half absent, the other half still trailing the last look he had of the woman. "I figure if I'm flying, I'm already in trouble with the surgeon general."

Kane hands over his credit card.

"Seating preference?"

"Not a one," Kane says.

"Luggage to check through?"

"Nope," Kane says.

"Excuse me," he says, "but that woman that was just here a moment ago, the very attractive one. It's embarrassing, but I think I know her. It's not possible that she's going to be on the same flight, is it?"

The salesgirl looks up knowingly. She smiles--but it is not the smile she's been taught to deliver in her ticket-agent training.

Kane grins. "Ah, come on," he says. "Give me a break, huh?"

"You're in luck," the salesgirl says, looking back down at her work again. When she at last looks up to give Kane his ticket and receipt, she says, "Thank you, sir--have a good flight. Eighty four boards in twenty minutes at Gate 10," and then, without the least change in her expression, she adds in a less professional voice, "From the look of you, I'd say she's in luck herself."

"I love you too," Kane says.

He pockets his ticket, and strides quickly off to the bank of telephone booths. He takes the first booth,

breathes wearily, sits down, and rummages among the change in the pocket of
the rumpled blue seersucker sport coat
he's wearing. He finds a dime and then
he pulls out of the sport coat, folds it
carelessly in half and stuffs it between
the shelf and the telephone box.

He tries Nat again. No answer.

He yanks the sport coat loose and
gets out a cigarette, the bulky brass
lighter.

Michael starts to dial Elaine. He
really ought to tell her he is leaving
town, he thinks. Denise's loveliness
clouds his vision for the moment.

"Aw shit," he says out loud to no one
in particular. "I'd only get an argument!"

He hangs up, collects his things, and
leaves the booth.

Michael cannot put his finger on just
what this quality is that Elaine possesses
that serves to make him so angry when
she is not even present nor uttered a
word.

The guard says, "Empty your pockets, please." The guard says, "Just
put everything into this plastic bucket,
please--keys, coins, everything."

The guard says this very mildly,
very politely, his courtesy unimpeach-
able, a genial professional in pursuit of

his orderly daily routine. And even though Kane does precisely as he is asked to do, he knows that if the sonof- abitch says one more thing, asks one more question, no matter how reason- able, no matter how perfectly in order, Kane will tear the bastard down to the ground--one fucking brick at a time.

Los Angeles Suburb

It was his wife Linda who talked him out of the Japan offer, arguing that it would put them just that much farther from Michael, never knowing that it would also create the occasion to end the affair David was in. Or perhaps she did know. Is it possible she wanted him to stay with it? It was not difficult to imagine what her reasons might have been. An affair of her own, perhaps, or simple weariness with the sagas of bed, matrimonial or otherwise. David supposed it was not uncommon in a wo- man of forty-eight, despite the popular notions on the subject. God knows, nor is it uncommon with men. One tires so quickly of the flesh he thought--of one's own and everyone else's -the flows, the weight, the ceaseless human complication no matter how clear-headedly one enters into such things.

David had not planned to have an

affair, to get involved again. It had been five years since his last affair. He remembered it well but not of his own choosing. Scenes from the tempestuous encounters and flashbacks of Anne's uncommonly beautiful face haunted him still at odd and unplanned times. They still disturbed and aroused him even now as no other before or after. Not his wife. No one. But Anne had been his pupil and was so much younger than he and they had no other mutuality beside science and their sexuality. None. Neither of them could comprehend what made the other tick or what each other's needs were--aside from the biological. It had been a strange and almost bizarre relationship. David Kane could not identify the root causes. Was it he? Or was it she? Or was it just how they were together? No matter the why, all other women paled by comparison and for five years he avoided all encounters. Even this time in fact he tried not to be involved. But not out of some absurd principle of marital fidelity. To remain faithful to Linda for conscience's sake or because he owed her such behavior? Nonsense. It was just that it was too much trouble. Dr. David Kane felt that one owes people nothing! One's debt is entirely to things more enduring than

people. Ideas, one's work, the expan-
sion of knowledge, perhaps--in the ab-
stract, to mankind, to the human species
perhaps--but not to this person or that
person, one's wife, one's parents, one's
children, and so on. And his lover, did
he owe her anything beyond the touch of
his body against hers? It was payment
enough.

David felt that people should realize
that the time he gives them is all he
needs to give them--his most precious
coin of exchange. All else is limit-
less--but time, human time, is the only
exhaustible commodity.

In any event, and for whatever real
reason, Linda said don't go, and thus he
didn't.

"You understand," David said, "what
it would mean for us. How we would
live over there--like virtual lords."

She smiled slightly. He remembers
they were sitting on the patio, having a
late Sunday breakfast. It was magnificent that day--October, early November,
the vaguest chill in the air, enough to
have put them both in Shetlands and
corduroy trousers. Linda sat facing out
toward the rose garden, so that she was
more or less turned to him in profile,
and when she smiled he saw how the
creases that bracketed her lips had

deepened somewhat. From what? The hardening of the small face muscles over the years, the skin less supple now that it was giving up its moisture, the etching effect of the sun, bitterness?

God, but she was still a handsome woman--very possibly more lovely than when he had married her twenty-nine years ago. Auburn hair, patrician face, good bones. He supposes it is the secret to lasting beauty in human beings, the hard structure beneath. Yes, she might have had a lover. What man would not want her?

"Does that amuse you?" he said.

"A little," she said, and with the backs of her fingers she flicked at some crumbs that had caught on a fold on her sweater.

"There's nothing wrong with living like a lord," he said. "Haven't I earned it?"

She did not turn to face him, but she raised her voice as if to make certain the roses heard.

"Of course, you have, darling. It's just that there was a time when you thought such things--well, trifling, even a little despicable."

"I'm older now," he said. "Age alters attitudes."

She turned to face him, her eyes

narrowing against the force of the sun that flared from behind him.

"Yes, doesn't it?" she said.

He said nothing in reply. When she reached to the table for her cigarettes, he poured her more coffee and freshened his own cup, and then he got to his feet.

"Just going to take a turn around the grounds," he said. "Stay here. Wait for me. We'll talk when I get back."

"No," she said.

"The sun will do you good. I won't be but a minute."

"No," she said, her voice distant again. "It's Sunday, and I want to call Michael before he goes out."

"Before they go out."

She fluttered her hand in front of her face as if brushing away an unseen insect.

"Yes, of course," she said. "I always try to chat with Elaine too."

David glanced at his watch. "It's already after one in New York, so if you intend to reach Michael--"

She looked up sharply, a length of coppery hair catching in the gentle wind that was blowing down from the foothills.

"I don't suppose you would like to speak with Michael?"

David Kane turned away and strode

toward the kennels at the side of the house. He didn't look around, but he knew she would still be sitting there, struggling against the impulse to hurry inside.

The dogs threw himself at the fence and fell into a fit of barking as soon as they heard his footsteps. "Hey, old fellows!" He called, but his attention was in a thousand other places--until the myriad images melded into one image, the ivory face of a chestnut-haired woman, her wash of hair spilled behind her against the field of a lemon-colored pillowcase, a fine misting of perspiration glinting in the hollows under her large, closed eyes. It was Anne.

He could feel her body trembling beneath his.

"What?" He had whispered, his lips over hers. "What is it?"

But she only shook her head.

"What?" He said. "Tell me."

Her eyelids lifted and then they again slowly closed.

How strange it was, the way she had finally answered--not with daring or satisfaction, but as if she were delivering a declaration of utterly colorless fact, a statement of purely impersonal observation, very like how he himself must sound when he is busy at his desk in the lab.

"It's this," she said, whispering. "It's that barring the possibility you underwent a vasectomy while you were lecturing in Oslo last week, you and I have just accomplished an act of conception, David. Do you understand, David? Like it or not, you are going to be a father again."

Miami Beach, 10:00 A.M.

Nathan Kane had slept the sleep of the exhausted. The medication had sent him into a deep slumber, an odyssey during which he had glimpsed the face of every person he had ever known and revisited every familiar spot. The journey through time and space had been a kaleidoscope of color and voices but now all the sound and fury and motion had stopped. All was still. The giant body is stirring now, the heavy eyelids struggling to open.

The shadows begin to take form and substance, materializing into one large dark man and one small light man at the foot of his bed. Friday and Goldmesser are standing there watching the old man carefully.

"So, boychik!" the little man cries. "Still Alive? I thought you might have kicked the bucket on us. There must still be some abuse left in you that has to get out before you die."

The old man yawns and stretches his mighty arms. "Goldmesser, you still here? Friday, throw the puny bastard out!"

The little man smiles.

"Now that I know you're feeling better I can leave on my own accord."

Friday interjects defensively.

"You shouldn't ought to talk to Mr. Goldmesser like that, Mr. Kane. He probably saved your life by coming by when he did."

"Nonsense! I'm not going to be beholden and obligated to a former ladies garment manufacturer who would never negotiate in good faith." When he senses the rath of protest about to come from this incongruous team of Goldmesser and Friday, Nathan waves his arms and mellows.

"O.K., O.K., let bygones be bygones. Thank you very much for whatever you have done for me, Goldmesser" then hastens to add "but don't expect any favors in return."

"None expected, don't worry. So now I'll run along. The little woman is waiting. I will leave you in Friday's care. If you need anything, give a holler, all right?"

The old man waves him out.

"Go already!"

When the door closes Friday comes close to Nathan.

"Seriously, how do you feel, Mr. Kane?"

The twinkle is back in the old man's eye.

"How should I feel? Great! Had a little too much sun because of that fascist policeman, that's all."

"Are you sure, boss?"

"Wanna arm wrestle?"

The old man springs from the bed to a sitting position, placing his right arm in position.

"Come on! Two out of three falls. What do you say?"

Friday smiles.

"O.K. Mr. Kane, maybe later. But first I want to have a serious talk with you."

The old man draws himself up to a standing position, stretching himself out to his full immense height, eyeball to eyeball with the equally tall Friday.

"Now just a minute, Boy, since when does a black slave have serious talks with his lord and master?"

Impatiently, Friday mocks the old man's overly theatrical voice.

"Now cut that crap out, Mr Kane,

That baloney is for the public. There's nobody here now except you and me."

Resignedly, the old man sighs and sits down in a white lounge chair.

"O.K. soul brother, speak. What's on your mind?"

"I want to know what that shooting was all about, that's what!"

Nathan Kane scoffs.

"Oh that, that was nothing. I was hoping something like that would happen."

Friday throws his arms into the air and paces the floor in obvious agitation.

"This is a dangerous game you are playing, old man. You could get hurt--hurt real bad."

"What do you care?"

"You know you don't mean that, Mr. Kane. You are making my job real tough. Plus you are making me a sitting duck in a pond right along side of you--inviting target practice--and you and me are pretty big targets."

"You afraid to die, Friday? You were born to die--just like me."

"Not before my time--if I can help it. And not as bait in a silly game that a crazy old man is playing."

"What game? What is this about a game? I'm writing my memoirs--cleansing my tarnished soul before I die, just an errant Israelite making ready to meet my maker."

"BULL!--and double Bull! I know your devious mind. Now two can play a game. If you don't level with me, I'll tell the whole world what your real secret is."

Nathan Kane assumes a wounded expression, and boylike, as if butter would not melt in his mouth.

"Secret? Who has secrets? What secret are you going to tell--the whole world yet?"

Friday mimics the old man.

"I'll tell everybody that you are my real father."

"Wha-a-a-a-t?" Nathan roars.

The ringing of the phone interrupts the heated exchange.

The old man's face lights up like a christmas tree and he yells exultantly:

"I'll bet that's Michael!"

Friday uses his best southern butler voice:

"Kane residence."

"Who may I say is calling?"

"One moment please. I will see if Mr. Kane is available to speak with you, sir."

The old man's face falls.

"It's not Michael?"

Friday holds his palm over the mouth

piece.

"It's your publisher, Mr. Richmond, calling long distance from New York. Do you want to talk to him?

"Sure, why not. Let me have the phone."

"Hello, Steve, how are you?"

The voice at the other end is rapid, the words spilling out excitedly.

"I'm fine, Nat. How are you? The first tape is dynamite--of the nuclear variety. It will blow them out of their pants."

"That's nice, Steve. I'm glad you like it."

"Like it? I love it. When can I have the next tape? This week?"

Nathan Kane laughs.

"Hold your horses, Steve. I'm an old man. I have to go at a slow pace. I know you got the publicity out that Nathan Kane was finally telling his story, right?"

"How did you know, Nat? Did you see a copy of the Book Digest?"

"No, but I got a calling card from one of the readers who isn't too thrilled with the whole idea. They shot at me today, Steve."

"Shot at you? Oh my God. Are you all right, Nat?"

"I'm fine. They missed. I'm sure

they meant to miss. It was a warning. They don't want me to go on with it."

"So what are you going to do, Nat?"

"I'm working on the next tape, Steve. You'll get it in a week or so."

"Nat?"

"Yeah, Steve?"

"There's no way of telling how many persons you are liable to scare, is there."

The old man thought for a moment.

"You have a point, Steve. There might be a whole army of hit-men looking for me."

"Maybe we ought to call it off."

There was anger in Nathan Kane's voice.

"Not on your life--or mine! Don't you dare!"

"O.K. Be careful will you?"

"I'll be all right. I have Friday to protect me."

"Maybe I ought to send you another body guard. What do you think Nat?"

"I don't need anybody. Don't worry, I'll be all right."

The old man hands Friday the phone to return to its cradle and then collapses in a heap to the floor. Nathan Kane was not the Nathan Kane of old.

Kane opens his eyes and sees the bookends first. He does not move his

head.   He is not sure he could if he
tried.   He lets his eyes, the lids barely
raised, rest where chance put them--on
the bookends, on the two conscientious
fellows in bronze, absorbed forever by
blank pages they never turn.

The bookends consisted of two boys
modeled in bronze, both puckish fellows
to judge from the cast of their jaunty
boaters--but, ah, serious, scholarly lads
in truth.   For look!   See how each wise
boy has his knees hiked up to form a
brace for the weighty tome that he in
such rapture studies.   And see the leg-
end emblazoned on the base of the one--
The Boy Who Reads--and on the other--
Is The Boy Who Leads.

What were they?   Weren't they a wonderful buy?   Fifteen dollars for the pair?
In 1937?   Rose picked them up on Allen
Street--for David's room when David was
what?   Ten?   Eleven?   Who can remember?   And who can remember how they
happen to reside here, these corny
bronze figurines, here in this outlandish
modern   apartment,   where   virtually
everything is recent and formica and
plastic and ridiculously expensive junk,
where there is scarcely an object in
sight to betray the texture of real lives
lived with real things, things bumped
and chipped and scarred, things that

add up to the things of a life.

But Nathan remembers. He remembers that his son never much cared for these sentimental bookends, although he took to heart the lesson they taught. Kane remembers the pride of the boy's mother to see these things, these bookends, getting farther and farther apart as the volumes her son so prized were added to the number between them. Then how did they get here, these studious boys? After all these years? Didn't they go off with David to college? Didn't they go off with the boy when he went off--to MIT and to Chicago and to Harvard? Or did he always leave them behind--for his mother to save year after year until now she's dead and here they still are, things bumped and chipped and scarred, standing on a white formica coffee table that stands, in turn, on a white acrylic carpet?

"Don't try to move. It's better if you just lie still for a while."

Whose voice? It is not Friday. There is someone sitting in the white chair that stands on the white carpet to the head of the white sofa Kane is lying on?

Kane says, "Who wants to move? I could sleep for a week."

"Go sleep," the voice says.

"You're a doctor?" Kane says. "Am I to understand these are medical instructions?"

"Mr. Kane, you make me tired," the voice answers--and at once Kane knows its master--Goldmesser.

No!

"What the hell are you doing in my house, Goldmesser!"

The reply is even-tempered and somewhat amused, the mild reasonable voice issuing from somewhere behind Kane's head.

"This is a house? Mr. Kane, you'll forgive me, but this is what you call an apartment. A very nice one, too--if I say so myself. The penthouse, aaahh-- the missus and me always wondered what gives up here. Nice. Meanwhile, enough pleasantries. Do yourself a favor for once in your life and rest. Go back to sleep."

Kane tries to pull himself up. He throws one large hand over the back of the sofa and grabs on. But it's no good--he hasn't the strength. He lets himself back down, and his hand and arm follow, dropping like dead weight.

"Out! Out of here, you miserable putz! This is private property! You weren't invited! Where the hell is Friday? You want me to get up from

here and call a cop?" Kane's rage is
directed at the ceiling. He hasn't even
got the strength to turn back into the
position he was in when he woke up, so
that he could at least shout at the coffee
table and maybe see the studious boys
raise their heads from their blank books.
But although Kane's indignation might be
sufficient to rouse bronze, it is scarcely
enough to ruffle the serenity of Mr.
Abraham Goldmesser, who sits quite
calmly in the high white chair, hunched
forward, the financial page of The Miami
Herald folded in quarters and spread out
on his short pillowy lap, his thick,
tortoise-shell eyeglasses tipped forward
onto the fleshy bulb of his shapeless
nose.

"You'll pardon me, Mr. Kane, Friday
is getting you some medication from the
pharmacy." Goldmesser speaks agree-
ably, his attention fixed closely on his
reading, "you know with policemen
you're not such hot stuff. Believe me,
a person couldn't help notice. To my
way of thinking, if you'll excuse the
observation, a fella who can't get along
with Officer Foley, such a perfectly civilized gent as that, that fella ain't got
a chance with your run-of-the-mill gen-
darme. So forget it. And as for me,
I'll leave when Friday returns. Don't

worry--so far as I'm concerned, it can't be too quick. You're no regular sweetheart, you know. Forgive me for saying this, my friend, but a living doll you're not."

Goldmesser laughs softly and uses his thumb to push his eyeglasses back into position.

Kane's voice is quieter now, but his tone makes up for it--all mocking nastiness, the mincing sarcasm plain.

"Forgive me. Excuse me. Pardon me. Jesus! Talk straight, man. Talk straight!"

"That's okay by me. Let's see, you owe me--as of now, two hundred smackers," Goldmesser announces. "That straight enough for you? A hundred to buy off the momser Foley. Another fifty I laid out for the prescriptions. Fifty more for the moron doctor we got in this building, who already took a little look at you and is calling a real doctor. How that Friday--strong as he is--got you up here I'll never know. Because the truth is, you're an ox, Mr. Kane. What you cost by the pound to carry in my opinion isn't worth it. But if you don't mind, you were a little too far out of it to consult at the time. So you'll forgive me, but I took a guess that you'd be willing I spent a bissel gelt to get you scraped off the sidewalk and <u>schlepped</u> back to your fancy residence here."

Kane says nothing. He is suddenly very dizzy again, and he closes his eyes--but the sofa continues to move beneath him, threatening to turn itself upside down.

"It's all right if I use the telephone? Mrs. Goldmesser worries she don't hear from me regular."

When there is no answer, Goldmesser rises, snaps the square of newspaper under his arm, and goes across the deep white carpet to dial the telephone. Where he stands now, he would be in Kane's line of vision if Kane were to open his eyes, but they stay shut as Kane tries to check the slow flipflop of the universe, the torpid reversal of up and down. As for Goldmesser's eyes, they rise to examine the four framed black-and-white photographs that are arranged in a tasteful pattern on the wall over the small white table that holds the telephone, also white. In one he sees Nathan Kane standing stiffly with Harry S. Truman, the dead President dwarfed alongside the leviathan in the heavy Irish tweed suit who has a cane pressed into the grass between his heavy English custom shoes. In another there is Kane and Roosevelt in a rowboat, both men in shirtsleeves and straw hats tilted rakishly and with cigarettes in holders stuck in their grinning faces. In a third, there's a staggeringly handsome boy of about seven sitting on a pony. In the fourth, there's a young man in baccalaureate cap and gown, the head turned in three-quarter profile, the face almost sardonically grave. There is an inscription in the lower right-hand corner of this fourth photograph. It reads: <u>For Nat, from his good buddy Michael. Keep 'em flyin', pal!</u>

"Make that two hundred and one dollars and twenty-seven cents, sweetheart," Goldmesser says as he dials. "I sent down to the commisary here in the building to replace you a dozen eggs. Jumbos. Anybody else, he'd fall on them, he'd break maybe half. But a <u>grobyan</u> like you? Every single <u>umglik</u> egg, <u>kaput</u>."

"Get out of my house! Friday! Where the hell are you? I have to get up! I have to finish my book. Where are my tapes? Goldmesser, I don't want you in here! Go home to your frumpy wife. Piss off, <u>putz</u>! Beat it!"

Goldmesser finishes dialing. He turns to Kane and smiles.

"Strike-breaker!   Scab!"   Kane shouts, eyes open now, the room spin-

ning, the little man holding the telephone now reduced to the size of a troll.
"Shmuts! Put down that telephone and
scram! Amscray, you punk! I want
you and your mealymouth and your nudnik doctors the hell out of here. Now!
I'll send you a check. Two hundred
and-one on the button!"

"And twenty-seven cents," Goldmesser says, not a jot less equably. "Esther? Esther, darling, it's Abe darling.
I'm up here in the penthouse with guess
who? The crazy gangster Kane. The
jerk finally keeled over in the street.
Who knows? The sun, a broken blood
vessel from yelling--go know. He says
somebody shot at him from a passing
car. Maybe he got scared. Nah! On
second thought nothing could scare him.
Why would they want to shoot him? An
angel like him--there are people waiting
in line to kill him if they could find him.
Besides it fell into his head to write a
book--an expose'. Who knows what secrets the old bastard knows that are going to make even more people nervous.
Meanwhile, a doctor's coming, so I'll wait
until they put him in a straitjacket or a
regular hospital. Besides, he owes me a
few bucks and I'm not leaving till I get
every dime. How bad off is he? To tell
you the truth, darling, if he dropped

dead this minute, I wouldn't be surprised. So, all right, you know where I
am."

Goldmesser hangs up and he laughs.

He looks at Kane and he says, "Do
me a favor and don't crap out on me
until you sign a check. Maybe you
should hurry up and tell me where your
fountain pen is, because you don't look
so hot to me, starker." Goldmesser
approaches the sofa. "So? The truth,
ox, how do you feel?"

"Don't call me that," Kane says, much
tamer now.

"What? Starker?"

"Ox."

"All right, I'll make an exception
since you're at death's door," Goldmesser says, smiling happily. "So? You
want to tell me how you feel?"

"For what?" Kane says. "In addition
to being a pain in the ass, you're also a
medical doctor?"

"Forget it," Goldmesser says, and
starts for the tall white chair behind
Kane's head.

"No," Kane says. "Wait a minute.
To tell you the truth, I don't feel so
hot."

"No kidding," Goldmesser says.
"Hey," the little man says, his eyes
twinkling behind his thick glasses. "I

never would have guessed it." But then he moves away to the head of the couch and out of Kane's vision, and when Kane sees Goldmesser again, the little man is pushing the tall white chair in front of him. He sits down, close to Kane's head. He says, "Take it easy. The doctor's going to get here any second, I promise. We also sent for an ambulance--but I didn't want to tell you so fast. It's downstairs waiting--just in case. You want me to get the house doctor back here? Actually, I think he's down there with the boys from the ambulance service. In two seconds, I could have him back. You want me to call the front desk and get the goniff up here?"

"No," Kane says, and then he shuts his mouth and he shuts his eyes on the rest of the sentence that's coming because there is something loose and flooding in him, and it is near to cresting and spilling out from all his openings. Kane squeezes. He is trying to hold on. There is a froth of gray light bubbling across his stomach, and in his ears everything hums. He feels himself careening, falling first to one side and then to the other. "Oh, good God!" Kane cries, and Goldmesser grabs his hand and lets Kane squeeze.

"I'll get the doctor," Goldmesser says, his voice still calm.

"No," Kane says. "Don't move," and Kane squeezes the little man's hand.

They stay this way for what seems a long time, but it is only seconds. For Kane it is an eternity, a pausing over a great ebony void that seems to be exerting intensifying pulses of suction and pressure as he hovers above it, his huge body lifting and lightly descending and then lifting again, a feather stalled on an indecisive wind.

At length Kane says something. He says, "I don't believe in God."

Goldmesser's voice is almost a whisper. "You want a medal for it?"

"I've killed men."

"So who hasn't?"

"I mean it," Kane says, his voice barely audible, the sweat standing out on his face now, the brown, leathery skin now bleached to a ghastly grey.

"All right," Goldmesser says.

"The first had that thing too--in the chin--like that twist of shit out there, the Nazi. What do you call it, like a crease?"

"Cleft," the little man says, trying to sustain his calm exterior.

"Cleft," Kane repeats tonelessly. "He was a Cossack. A sergeant. A police-

man who shit in my father's <u>yarmulke</u>.
Ivanov, the pig's name was Ivanov. He
had that thing in his chin."

"A cleft," Goldmesser says, his mind
racing for what to do, his heart cursing
the time this is taking.

"I was fourteen years old," Kane
says.

"God forgives you," Goldmesser says.

"There is no God," Kane says,
squeezing very hard now, his eyes
opening a little to see if he is still alive.
Perhaps to see the bronze dreamers one
last time. "Michael," the old man says.
"Rose. David."

The names are uttered as if they con-
stitute a prayer of some kind. Goldmesser hears this, and he feels himself close
to weeping. "Hold on," the little man
says, his small hand numb inside Kane's
great callused grip. But then the big
man's hand goes abruptly limp, the force
leaking suddenly out, the strength sur-
rendered, gone.

Goldmesser can feel it now, his own
hot sweat, the old man's. It is cold.

The little man just sits there. He
does not slip his hand from inside the
big man's huge hard palm. He just sits
there, watching, waiting--his lips moving
prayerfully. But what he is noiselessly
intoning is no prayer to him at all.

"Michael.   Rose.   David."

# # # #

New York, 10:30 A.M.

Michael is in luck. At least half the seats in the Gate 10 waiting area are unoccupied, and there is an empty space in the row of seats directly opposite Denise.

Kane takes it. He slumps down, stretches out his long legs, adjusts the toiletry items stuffed in his coat pockets, folds his arms, and looks around for the children. He sees them at the floor-to-ceiling window, absorbed in mute appreciation of the aircraft that is parked and waiting to take on passengers. The little girl has a happy face now and her brother is obviously her twin counterpart. Michael looks across at Denise and smiles. He is stunned when the woman calls across the space between them: "Michael Kane, you look like absolute hell."

Michael is amazed! She is not even surprised to see him!

He is so disarmed, that he stammers out his reply.

"No kidding. I do?"

"Awful," Denise says, her voice friendly and apparently sincerely con-

cerned. It is a lovely voice, full-bod-
ied, and controlled, and very penetrating. "Actually, the way you look, I'd
say you were a public menace. Women
and children should be given fair warning."

Kane sits up. This is incredible.

"Yeah," he says. "Like may be I
should wear a sort of sign, you know?
Something to give the faint of heart a
head start. A chance to beat it before I
look 'em in the eye."

"I am not faint of heart," the woman
says, not smiling so much now, her eyes
driving at Kane, her manner challenging, bold.

"No, I guess you're not," Kane says,
rising, getting to his full height, which
is great, and covering the few steps
that it takes to cross the little distance
and sit down beside her. "What the hell
are you doing here? You are not even
surprised to see me! You knew I would
be here, didn't you?" Kane says. "So
it looks like you have the advantage of
me. How about you level with me and
tell me exactly who and what you are?"

"Oh no," the woman says, not looking
at Michael but instead looking across the
room to where the children stand staring
out through the observation glass.
"That would be telling." She turns

away from the children, but still she does not look at Michael. She leans prettily forward and gathers the strap of her handsome leather satchel up into a loop and lifts the thing onto her lap, and then she stands. "I think I like it better this way," she says, turning to regard Michael. "Cindy!" the woman calls, moving a pace or two away from Kane. "Barry? Get ready, children-- we're going to board very soon!" She swings around gracefully and looks back at Michael. He is perplexed and con- fused--her manner enigmatic. Is this the same woman he has spent a glorious night with and only left a few hours ago? He sees how she has, in her artful pivoting, positioned her feet as would a dancer poised for applause. He looks at the bright slender red straps that criss- cross over her narrow naked feet, and then he slowly, very tellingly, moves his worshipful inquiry up the startling column of her tall body--legs, hips, waist, breasts--until his eyes are looking at hers. Denise returns Michael's mind- less gaze, the exchange promptly plum- meting into a profound mutuality. There is a queer, difficult silence, a kind of gluey thickening of the air between them as if it is moistened with rising copula- tory vapors. Denise removes her turban and gives her head an extravagant shake. The golden spill of her miraculous hair swims from one side to the other and back again, the light from the airport windows behind her catching at the frame that surrounds her face and turning its color from light brown to gold.

"Your seat number," the woman says. "What is it?"

Kane almost blanches. What is happening here is beyond reckoning, more dreamlike by the instant. This woman, this vision, who in the course of one unforgettable evening had awakened feelings and passions he had never known with Elaine or any other woman, was playing a game of hide and seek with him. She beckons him on--then draws the curtain of familiarity--then leaves it parted enough to lead him on. What is she up to--this at once magnificent yet mysterious siren. Is it just a game or method to her madness--or the thought occurs but briefly--just madness? It seems to Michael that their lives are criss-crossing of a purpose--by some grand design. But there is also biological chemistry at work here beyond the reasoning of design. This breathtaking woman is drawing him to her, magnetically, her body and voice calling, beckoning. She is like some matchless figure made manifest from the drifting, creamy stuff of purest male fantasy-seductive angel or angelic seductress, it hardly matters which--her slim arm lifting, one tapering finger opening out to him and then curling back to her breast in a lucent arc, the glowing lips parted to let pass one clear, murmured word:

Come. She repeats: "Your seat number?"

"Hell, I don't know," Kane says, his voice faraway, drugged, as if he speaks across distances a coma has created. "Let me look."

When he tells her, she says, "Not really. But how utterly quaint. The famous Michael Kane travels tourist class?"

"Yeah, well," Kane says, "I can fix that." He gets up. "Let's see your ticket." He holds out his hand, gazing down at the woman's hair as she lowers her head. He waits while she fishes in the depths of her carry-all, aware of what has happened to him, all thought of Elaine erased and the purpose of his mission to Miami and Nat temporarily having vanished from the forefront of his mind. He realizes that something extraordinary has been overtaking him, that he is entirely here, entirely with this woman, his consciousness alive to

nothing save this creature's every gesture, her every word. When she places
the envelope containing her flight tickets
in his hand, it is like a sacrament, a
bottomless communing, nuptial, subtly
thrilling.

They are just announcing the boarding of the first-class cabin as Michael
starts for the gate stewards to see if he
can make the arrangements. He hears
the woman calling, "Cindy! Barry!" as
he gets in line with the passengers
queued up for check-in. It is then that
he thinks to flip open the envelope and
look for the name. The first ticket
reads Kessler, M., the second Kessler,
T., and the third Steiner, D.

Steiner? D. Steiner? Denise! And
the children--Kessler?

Divorce, Michael thinks, believing he
has the answer. Divorce can be an ending or a beginning. Before he had met
Denise he had already known in his
bones that Elaine and he had come to the
parting of their ways. Now there was
Denise and there was that excitement
and energy of feeling that had so long
been absent from his life.

Michael made the seat exchange without incident and the four of them board-
ed seemingly like a normal--but excep-
tionally attractive family group. They

are seated next to each other in the forward cabin of the aircraft. Denise in the window seat, Michael on the aisle. She pulls herself up to lean over the seatbacks in front of her. She busies herself with the two children sitting there, headsets already plugged into their ears as each child switches from channel to channel more in search of the miracle of stereo than of anything else. Kane yields himself to the view that she gives him, the white of her T-shirt drawn tight to her back so that the thin line of her brassiere strap shows, its very thinness testimony to the fact that the bearing of two children has not deteriorated her breasts to the point where greater support is needed. He marvels at this, the obviously firm breasts and buttocks, their tissue still springy, resilient, their quality unaffected by maternity or time.

When the woman sits back and looks at him, she seems not at all curious to learn how Michael happens to be on this plane. But if she asked, could and would Michael explain? Or does she already know--Ah--how could she know? Yet she somehow knew he would be here whether she knew his purpose or not. And when Kane inquired how this was so, her reply was teasing, an evasion.

He is about to ask her again when the
engines blast into full throttle and the
great lumbering giant starts its slow,
powerful run along the tarmac. Instead
Michael saves the question. Instead he
lets himself back against the seat and
yanks his safety belt as tight as it will
go. He is content to leave everything in
silence, to let the hazy moment move
ceaselessly forward, their two bodies
side by side as the aircraft hurtles on-
ward and then jumps impossibly free of
the rushing ground, a clumsy beast
now become the lightest of birds, all
gracefulness as it lifts and lifts into the
sailing air and settles on its course into
the long climb up to cruising altitude.

When the NO SMOKING sign winks
off, the woman takes a cigarette from
the pack she has been holding at the
ready. She raises the pack for Michael
to take one too. Michael does, a little
surprised to see that they are unfil-
tered--Lucky Strike, in fact. Aside
from Nat and his stubborn loyalty to
Camels, Kane has never come across
anyone who still smokes the more lethal
brands. She waits for him to give her a
light, her eyes on his as he digs in his
pockets for the heavy brass lighter. He
holds the flame to her cigarette and then
moves it to his, and when she puts down

the pack of Lucky Strikes on the wide armrest between them, Kane sets the big brass lighter squarely on top of it. The woman puffs on her cigarette, expelling the smoke from her delicate nostrils in a long, thin stream, her eyes considering the suggestive arrangement Kane's made, his heavy lighter atop her pack of cigarettes.

She looks up at him.

"That's all right," she says.

Michael says nothing. He is finding it difficult to speak in this woman's presence. It is as if he must invent a language, as if every word that occurs to him is untried and must be considered carefully before its use is dared. He has known her body and its sexuality, but he did not know the person within.

"Denise," he says, as if this were a code word that imparted pages and pages of meaning.

"Yes," the woman says, "that's right. And you are Michael."

Michael can't stop himself. He helplessly nods.

"Michael," he says, his voice hoarse, as if he has labored with the effort to heave these two syllables into view before her.

She looks away from him. She turns away and looks out the window. But

Michael can hear her very plainly when she speaks.

"Michael," she says. "Wasn't there an angel named Michael? Yes, I think so. Winged Michael travels light. Of course. But Denise--" She turns back to him and finds his eyes. "Denise is traveling, how shall I say? Heavy?"

Her motion almost makes him jump. She reaches her hand to his and lightly grasps his fingers.

"Shall I tell you how heavy I travel, dear Michael, now that we are air-borne?

Michael stares. Is he dreaming this? Is this actually happening?

"I travel with the greatest of all weight, a piece of baggage whose burden is too fabulous for any scale." She is looking into his eyes, her soft cool hand gently closing tighter on his fingers. "A bomb, dear Michael. A bomb."

Kane's jaw drops open--but then he quickly laughs.

"A bomb?" he says. "You say you've got a bomb with you"

"Hush, dearest," the woman says, and releasing his hand, she raises two fingers to his hips and briefly presses them closed, all of this accomplished with such broad theatricality that Michael is not certain if she is seeking laughter or applause.

"Well," he says, relaxing now, willing to go along with the joke for as long as she wants, "that's really a terrific coincidence, you know. Because, like I've got one too."

"Good," the woman says, turning back to look out the window again.

"Yeah, that's okay," Michael says, leaning over to her, his voice comically conspiratorial now, his mouth almost touching her hair. "That way if mine doesn't go off, we've always got yours for a back-up, right?"

But the woman does not answer. She stays that way for a time, her head turned away to the view out the window. At length, Michael sits back deciding that he will hit the washroom and see to himself as soon as the seatbelt sign goes off. But he doesn't go. He feels her breath on his check, the distinct scent of the lavender fragrance that she wears so palpable that it is like something his skin feels too.

"We are going to die together, darling."

Michael gapes. He tries to check his expression, to fashion up some equally farcical reply, something to match her melodramatic horseplay. But first, my dearest, one kiss or My passion, my beloved, this world is too cruel or perhaps

a wink and <u>Well, toots, I haven't had a</u>
<u>better offer all day</u>. But nothing suit-
ably in keeping with the high mark of
her theatre comes to him soon enough,
and by the time something does, Denise
has snapped open her safety belt and is
leaning through between the seatbacks in
front and talking to the children.

Michael listens to her closely, sifting
for signs. Her voice is cheerful but
businesslike, as if she herself is a
stewardess much accustomed to these
routine attentions.

"Lunch will be served shortly, sweet-
hearts. Are your little tummies just
starving?"

Michael can tell that she is fiddling
with things up there, tightening seat-
belts or getting headsets securely back
in place. Michael is ready with his line
when she returns to her place. But the
woman breathes a loud satisfied sigh,
looks at him, and speaks first. "And
you?" she says, smiling sympathetically,
professionally, "Is your little tummy just
starving too? Or is it only your big Jew
cock that is too hungry for words?"

<u>Harvard</u>   (Some Years Back)
Anne was superb in the laboratory,
truly superb. She'd been one of the
two Radcliffe girls to audit Dr. David

Kane's Saturday morning seminar in theoretical genetics, a series of speculations he offered during his last year at Harvard to anyone who wished to attend. In order to keep away those of merely playful intent, he locked the door precisely at seven-thirty. Whoever was not in the room by that time of the morning of the first meeting was thereafter excluded from further meetings, a rule that obtained for all other meetings as well. Be late for one, any one, and you were denied access to all subsequent meetings--a strict and arbitrary policy, to be sure, but just as surely it proved the most efficient way to weed out those who were less than genuinely committed to the pursuit of the ideas that concerned him at the time.

Anne was there that first morning, and all succeeding mornings--and she was invariably the first to arrive. In fact, as David remembers it, her arrival was, without exception, prior even to his. He would come through the door, to find her seated in the same chair, always the same chair, the one that stood immediately to the right of the place he characteristically favored, her sleek brown hair glinting in the burnished light that came like sheets of golden rain through the angled blinds.

In the time that remained before the
start of the seminar, the two of them
would sit in silence as other persons put
in their bustling appearance, out of
breath from the haste they'd made from
bed to hurried breakfast to the room
where David's public meditations were to
take place. It was difficult for David,
sitting like that--waiting in the stillness,
just the two of them locked in silence
until they were joined by some lively
third party. Sometimes they would be
alone for seconds, sometimes for minutes, always in that haunting silence
which instantly erupted between them.
He would seat himself, take out the
scrap of paper on which he had jotted
some note or two, promptings of a
certain line of inquiry he wished to take
up that morning. He would place the
paper on the table before him, glance at
the words or symbols he'd scribbled over
coffee and then look up at her, always
expecting to find her head bowed in
respectful girlish deference. But it
wasn't--never once did he find her gaze
on other than his own eyes as he raised
them from that piece of notepaper.

She stared at him--with an utterly
disarming frankness, her lovely face
openly engaged in sustaining the reply
he made with his own eyes. It was

staggering, the power of the look she turned on him, her eyes unflinching in their excruciating encounter with his. The effect was inexpressibly sexual, the more so because they spoke not a word to each other. Eventually, he would always be the first to look away, his attention inevitably straying to some unfocused region of her bodice, a sector of the notable convexity of one of her breasts, a swatch of the soft brown fabric of the smock-like dress she routinely wore, sometimes the beige wool of the cardigan she held about her shoulders as the mornings moved from autumn to winter.

When the seminar reconvened after the mid-year holiday, the inevitable commenced in earnest. They used shabby motel rooms until he arranged for her to have a tiny apartment off campus. That summer, when Linda and Michael and David went as always to the house they then kept at the Vineyard, she took a modest loft in the nearby town of Chilton. When he joined the faculty at Cal Tech, she followed him to Pasadena and became a doctoral candidate under his direct supervision, and at Stanford she assumed the role of executive administrator in his lab, overseeing the other young scientists and managing to spare

him much of the paperwork, yet still
finding time to do important science in
her own right, particularly insofar as
she was increasingly interested in certain technical innovations.   In the laboratory, she was supremely gifted.   In
bed, she seemed to be entirely in control
of her passion, and for some extraordinary reason this made her even more
desirable.

Her sexuality, considerable as it was,
was virtually abstract--an aura she
gathered about herself with the speech
that issued so softly, but tellingly, from
her eyes.   Her allure was immense--a
quiet lustrousness, a virginal austerity
that was always without blemish no matter how many times David had already
entered her body and made it thrash in
violent climax.

That first morning--after the mid-
year holiday--when it was agreed between them, the thing acknowledged, it
had happened in a manner he then
thought so strange, yet now thinks so
altogether natural.

Everyone else had left the room.   He
was still sitting there, idly curling the
slip of paper between his fingers, rolling
it in on itself into a tight little tube, his
mind unwilling to let go of the thread he
had been teasing out into the open

during the course of the morning's dis-
cussion. When he at last looked up, he
saw her gaze waiting for him, her wide
eyes presenting themselves as if they
were her genitals set out on naked display. He remembers thinking that he
should look away now, that he must let
his eyes drift to the watery cascade of
her hair or to some safe, unanswering
region of her clothing.

The stillness in the room was like a
roar in his ears.

"Come," she said, not moving.
"Come, Dr. Kane," she said, and this
time they both stood up, moving in what
seemed a kind of mindless tandem.

They took a taxi. All the way there,
they never touched once. Nor did they
speak again--at least not to each other--
until he had locked the door of the motel
room behind them. Again she said,
"Come," as she stood across from him,
and then she turned and very gradually
drew down the chenille coverlet that lay
carelessly thrown across the bed. What
followed was sheer ecstasy.

Miami Beach, 11:00 A.M.

For some time now there has been no
sound in this room except for the slow
heavy cadence of the old man's breathing. The odd couple, the tiny Goldmes-

ser and mammoth Friday, have maintained a silent vigil waiting for the sleeping walrus to waken. When the phone rings in the next room they both move as one to answer it, but Goldmesser yields to Friday's bulk and speed. When Friday returns in a moment the little man gives him a questioning look.

"It was his publisher," Friday whispers. "I told him Mr. Kane would get back to him."

The two hardly had a moment to resume their patient watching when the phone rings again. This time Goldmesser is the first to pick it up but Friday is at his elbow.

"There is a man in the lobby with a package for Mr. Kane. He insists on bringing it up here. What do you think, Friday?"

"Tell him I will be right down there."

Friday leaves and Goldmesser returns to his place at Nathan's bedside.

"So what was that?" the old man says, his eyes closed, his face still turned into the pillow.

"My wife," Goldmesser says. "God bless her, she can't get enough of me."

"Mine's gone now," Kane says, a kind of exhaustion in his voice.

"May she rest in peace," the little man says.

"She suffered," Kane says.

"You should sleep," Goldmesser says.

"Who can sleep? Poor Rose couldn't stand what went on between me and the boy."

"And Michael?" Goldmesser says.

Kane's eyes open abruptly.

"Is Michael here?" the old may says, and he seems about to try to rise. "The kid's here?"

"No, no, no," Goldmesser says. "You must have been dozing. I only meant was the trouble between you and Michael?"

"Michael," the old man says, his face softening. "Ah, God in heaven, how I love that boy. Michael's me--the same." Nathan raises his arm and makes a fist. "The same. Like that."

"Trouble with your son, you mean," the little man says, his voice coaxing, urging things out.

"David. To David too, that's what I was--the ox. A brute."

"Too?" Goldmesser says, pulling at something, gently easing something out, drawing forth what wants to come.

Nathan looks at Goldmesser but does not respond to this. Instead he asks.

"Where's Friday? How come he left me with you?"

"It's all right. Relax. He only went

down to the lobby. There's a man there who has a package to deliver to you. He wanted to come up. But Friday said no--he would go down."

The old man smiles.

"That Friday is all right. He's got brains. He'll check him and that package out good. Leave it to him."

"May I ask--if I'm not intruding--how did you happen to get such a schvarzer for a manservant?"

"You too?" The old man's voice is rising. "You are intruding! I haven't told him yet so why should I tell you? He thinks I'm his real father. Now no remarks--or tired as I am--I'll break you in half!"

Goldmesser's voice is patronizing.

"If size alone were the sole judge, it would be a possibility."

"Everybody wants something from me except my son. My publisher wants his book and--."

"By the way he just called."

"--Friday wants to know who he is and God only knows what you want, Goldmesser."

"I don't want anything--except to see you back on your feet. That's all!"

There is a loud sigh and then a pause.

"I'm tired," Nathan says.

"Of course. It's good. Let go. It's better."

"Let go of what?" Nathan says, his voice stronger now. "Of life?"

"I meant feelings," Goldmesser says. "The tsimis that's in you. Get it out."

"Help me sit up," the old man says.

Even with Nathan's help, Goldmesser must struggle to get the big man up with his back comfortably against the headboard.

"Good?"

"Thanks," Nathan says.

"Don't mention it."

"Yeah, well, thanks for all of it," Nathan says. He raises his arms in front of him and studies the veins on the insides of his forearms, and then he lowers his arms to the bed.

"We were talking about who else called you the ox," the little man says, settling back in the chair he's drawn up close to the old man's bed.

Nathan looks at the little man and almost smiles. He breathes a large sigh and passes his hand over his eyes. "So be it," he says. "All right, nachshlepper," Nathan says, "I'm going to favor you with a little story for your troubles, a little something nobody's ever heard. You won't interrupt me? You won't pester me with your nudnik comments?

You'll just sit and you'll listen?"

"Mr. Kane," Goldmesser says, "when a fool is getting ready to meet his maker, I give him every consideration."

Nathan laughs, a choked sound that is followed by a spate of coughing. His face colors, a reddening as he struggles to catch his breath. Goldmesser stands to help him, to do something, but Kane waves the little man away.

"Listen," the big man says, straining to recapture his voice, "people get labeled, and once you get yours, that's the way it is from start to finish. But there's more. A lot more."

"I'm dying to learn," the little man says.

Kane lets himself back against the headboard.

He grumbles and then clears his throat.

"My father was the teacher in Horka. That's where I was born--in Russia."

Goldmesser nods, and closes his eyes.

"He was like me in size, maybe a few inches smaller all around. But big--and like me and my son and like Michael, the kid, the same color hair. Like gold. But that's where the likeness ends. He was a holy man, very inward--also a teacher. Hirsch. Hirsch Kapulkin. Hirsch Kapulkin of Horka--among the

Yiddim a very big man. Holy. With him, everything was rules. My mother, it doesn't matter. Who knew she was there? That's how much my father ruled. So we're talking about this Horka, an abomination for containing a few dozen families of abominated Jews. It's the usual picture. Except in Horka there was Ivanov, the Czar's officer, a sergeant. Every shtetl had its Czar's officer, but only Horka had Sergeant Ivanov. Not just a Cossack and a killer and a monster, but maybe the actual Devil. For the moment out there on that steaming sidewalk, I was sure he had returned in the person of Officer Foley. Anyway--and always on a white horse yet, mind you--and with black boots that shone like glass. It had to be--with both Ivanov and Hirsch Kapulkin there-- it was inevitable. So one day he comes to our place. Do you believe this? The man rode his white horse through the door. 'Jew!' he screams. 'Get your family!' And my father called us from the other room. Seven, counting us all and my mother, me the oldest, me up front--fourteen and already the size of my father and still growing. We stood there, the horse stamping, his feet cracking the frosted boards. It was winter. Ivanov up there on top of him, in furs, black furs--the boots like glass, a burly man, but not big. The face was--there is no other word for it--puggish. Nose like a snout, swept back, and the upper lip turned out to show the pink, wet flesh. Eyes crowded close, and in the chin that crease that went across. You call it a..."

"Cleft," Goldmesser again instructs, eyes still closed.

"Cleft," Kane's softened voice continues. "Deep, very deep. He screamed, 'Big Jews and little Jews! An assortment!' And then he dismounted. I don't remember everything just after that. There were--things. He touched us. He touched my mother. He fingered the fabric at her bodice. It was maybe just the rough stuff of shawls because we were swaddled, you see. Against the cold. But I remember his fingers there, and the glinty fire that came off his boots. Was my head cast down? I don't know. But then I heard him scream again. 'I give the biggest Jew a choice! Jew,' he shrieked at my father, 'show me your Jew thing, the filthy Jew worm that hangs from you there!' And with his swagger stick Ivanov poked between my father's legs. My father did nothing. He stood there. Ivanov screamed. He used his stick to jab and jab. My mother started to cry, and when that happened, the children too. It made Ivanov furious. 'Jews, Jews, always weeping! What troubles you, little Jews? You do no honor to the Czar's officer! Silence, silence, or I shove you all back where you came from." At this my father made as if to move. Did he really? Or did I imagine it? I don't know. I know the rest happened fast. Ivanov yanked out his revolver, a big black weapon, but shiny, 'Jews, Jews!' he screamed, 'Are you insane?' He was waving the big revolver and backing up, and when he fell against the horse, the animal stretched back its legs and spread them and urinated a powerful hissing stream, and into this there then dropped a succession of evil-smelling turds. I remember staring at the steam rising, and I don't know how long after that I saw the next thing, but it was Ivanov's hand, and in it he had my father's yarmulke, and he was reaching down to capture a turd inside it, and he was shrieking, 'Jew, pious Jew! How is it your head is uncovered? Hey, Jew, hey! The lice will get away! Here, Reb Kapulkin, cover your head! Hurry, good Jew! Make haste!' And in one hand Ivanov held the revolver and in

the other my father's yarmulke over-
turned with the boiling ingot of horse-
shit inside it. You understand, Goldmesser? You hear me? This is what I
saw."

"And you saw your father put it on,"
the little man murmurs, his eyes not
open to see Nathan Kane nod.

"Late that afternoon, my mother
asked my father to get wood from the
little forest for the fire, and my father
said, "No, not today, that it was better
to wait until the Cossack was tame
again, that the swine would be out there
still riding around. 'Tomorrow,' he
said, but my mother said 'Hirschele,
husband, the kinder--it's cold. Ahead
of us we have the night without wood,'
'No,' my father said, and put his face
back into a book. So I took my mother
aside, and I told her not to worry, that
I, Nochem, would go, that I, Nochem,
would get the ax and the rope and bring
back enough for the night, and my
mother said, 'Quiet! You will not!' And
this my father heard and said, 'Shut up,
woman, and let the ox go!' It was my
papa's name for me." Kane intoned, and
he passed his hand in front of his eyes
as he said it. "Ox. To him I was a
brute, a bovan, a thing good for anything so long as it was not prayer or

thought.   He   said   that   the   Cossack
would not hurt the ox, that he could not
hurt the ox, and when my mother protest-
ed,   my   father   screamed.   Just   like
Ivanov, he screamed. 'Silence, woman!
The house needs wood! The ox will go!'
So I took up the ax and looped the rope
around my waist, and I went out that
door and into the setting sun and into
the blazing cold. The forest was not far
off, fifty, a hundred yards from the
edge of--"

It is the telephone, its ragged signal
like a blade hacking at iron. Goldmesser
jumps from his chair. "I'll be back in a
minute," he says, and quickly makes his
way to the living room.

"Yes," he says, snatching the receiver up with both hands.

"Is this the Kane residence?" a man
says.

"Yes," Goldmesser answers. "Is this
he?"

"No it's a friend. He can't come to
the phone just now.

The caller speaks in a distinct cultur-
ed voice belying the words he is saying.

"Tell the old bastard to forget this
book he's writing or I'm going to splat-
ter him over the sidewalk. Are you
receiving my message?"

"Yes sir," Goldmesser says. "I hear

you loud and clear!   I'll tell him right away!"

"Some of his old friends regard this book as very unfriendly and want him to stop it now!   Tell him next time we won't miss!   Got it?"

"Got it!   Yes sir."

"Now, listen carefully!   I want to see an ad in the next edition of the New York Times Book section saying that Nathan Kane and his publisher have decided to scrap the project.   Do you understand?"

Goldmesser could hardly speak but he understood and he said so.

The caller parted with these words:

"Go tell him right now--every word--before you forget!"

"Right now!   Yes sir!"

Click!

Goldmesser fairly crawled back to the bedroom.   He abhorred violence or the threat of it.   Badly frightened by this voice that spoke so nicely yet said such terrible things, he stood at the old man's bedside trembling and tongue-tied.

"So who was it, Goldmesser?"   Nathan says.   "All of a sudden you don't look so good.   You want to lie down here next to me?"

Goldmesser composed himself quickly and declined with thanks.   Then he proceeded to tell Nathan exactly what the man said.

"That's great!" says Nathan to a stunned Goldmesser. "Can't you see? I have everybody's attention!"

"Is that what this foolishness with a book is all about?" Goldmesser asks increduously. "An old man who was once famous and is now out of the lime-light gets lonely so he wants attention by getting himself killed? You want to see your picture on the front page be-fore it gets to the obituary page, right?"

The old man shakes his head waving his arms vigorously as if he were fend-ing off a swarm of bees.

"You don't understand, you goddamn-ed strikebreaker! That's not it at all!"

"Well what the hell is it then?"

Before Nathan Kane can answer, the door bursts open and a bruised and bleeding Friday comes reeling in.

"What happened?" scream Nathan and Goldmesser in unison.

"It's O.K. Everything is all right--now!" Friday stands with his muscular back braced against a wall. His breath is heavy and labored. There is a nasty cut on his forehead that is oozing blood that he wipes away from his left eye.

"The sonofabitch had a bomb in the

package! Can you imagine? He expected me to just take the damned thing and
bring it up here and hand it over to Mr.
Kane and then all of us and the penthouse go boom into little pieces all over
the city."

"Oh, my God," Nathan Kane cries
out. "Somebody is really that scared? I
wouldn't have believed it. So where is
the guy and where is the bomb?"

"No more!" Friday says throwing his
arms up to the sky in an expression that
really required no other words.

"And you, Friday," says Goldmesser.
Come let me get you patched up."

"I'll be all right, thank you. I'm
going to run down to the first aid station. I just came up to tell you what
happened. Take good care of Mr. Kane
til I get back. O.K. Mr. Goldmesser?"

"Sure. Sure. I will." And then he
adds. "If it was attention you wanted,
it is attention you are getting, Nathan
Kane!"

Then he retakes his position at
bedside.

"So where were we?" Goldmesser
calls out brightly as he starts to go
back into the bedroom. "In your story
you were just getting to the forest with
that ax in your hand!"

Delta 84, 11:30 A.M.

Michael doesn't know what to worry about more--the bewildering woman or cutting himself. But he finishes shaving unmarked, and then there is nothing but the woman, this Denise, to absorb Kane's thoughts as he brushes his teeth and sprays warm water back through his long, brilliant hair. Yet it does Kane no good to try to think about her. What she does to him, the sheer effect of her thrilling physicality, her face, her body, her voice, explodes everything into chaos, makes thought impossible.

He tries to reach for some clear-headed measure of her. How much is caprice? How much is theatre? How much is design? How much is teasing? How does she happen to be on this plane with him? Is this business or pleasure or is pleasure her real business?

Kane stands looking at himself in the mirror, recollecting what she's said. How she's said it, in what sort of context this or that came up. A bomb? What brought that on? And the other thing, the wild thing she said just before he got up to come here and shave and brush his teeth. Where did that come from? Is Denise simply reacting chemically to something she instantly detected in Michael? Or is she playacting? Does she just think it's smart to be crazy, destructive, outrageous? Or is Denise just following some lead that Kane himself unknowingly established?

After the previous glorious night Michael is confused and perplexed. He remembers the last thing she said: "I hope this isn't going to be a one-night stand" and there was a genuine tear in her eye. Now the woman is a goddamn total enigma--but a very beautiful one. And her kids are in the middle of all this? Michael shakes his head and does not understand any of it. Thirty thousand feet above earth with a woman he desires with a wanting Michael Kane never believed possible?

But it's no good, no use--Kane cannot fathom it and he cannot keep any of it clear.

He drops the razor and the can of instant lather into the waste receptacle, and then he does the same with the toothpaste and toothbrush. He studies himself in the mirror. He says, "Who knows, maybe you're the crazy one." He buttons his collar, straightens and tightens his tie, gets back into his sport coat, pulls open the door, and smiles apologetically at the old woman waiting her turn.

He goes up the aisle toward the front

of the aircraft and the first-class cabin, feeling more himself now, more really awake now that he's undergone the ritual of getting himself in shape for the day.

"Well, now," Michael says, as he takes his seat next to Denise, "your bomb still ticking nicely?"

"Don't be a jerk," she says, turning to Kane and gently laying the cool palm of her hand against Kane's newly shaven cheek, her quick soft touch surprising him, exciting him. "Now you mustn't talk like that, darling," Denise says. "Don't you know it's unlawful to even joke about such a thing on an airplane?"

"Who's joking?" Kane says.

"That's precisely my point," she says. "Now do try to be a good little boy while I get you something to suck on and quiet you." She pokes around inside her leather satchel, presently producing a silver flask. She uncaps it and holds it out to Kane.

"What is it?" he says.

"What is it?" Denise says. "Um, let me see. Balm? Nectar? Oil of Disappearance?"

"Is it something mad bombers drink?"

"Oh, do be a dear and shut up," Denise says, raising the flask toward Michael's lips and smiling warmly.

He takes it from her and drinks,

plugging his tongue against the mouth of the flask so that just a sip gets by, but at the same time making reasonable swallowing motions.

"Good?"

"Yummy." He offers the flask back to her.

"Have more," she says. "It will improve the quality of your conversation."

"After you," Michael says, shaking his head and grinning, more unsure of everything by the minute, even willing to believe that he may have just sampled poison.

She takes the flask from him. But instead of drinking from it, she slots it between her thighs. Kane looks at the flask quesioningly, but the tightening of the denim against the woman's perfect flesh drives the question out of Michael's mind.

"All right," he says. "What <u>was</u> it? It tasted sweet."

"Honestly," Denise says, diving into her leather satchel again, "whatever it was, it certainly hasn't done a thing for your feeble powers of conversation." This time she produces an ebony cylinder from her handbag, popping apart its two sections and, with a deftness that Kane thinks extraordinarily feminine, the

woman applies to her lips, in swift practiced strokes, some kind of creamy
colorless gloss, a simple female ceremony
Denise accomplishes with such lovely
grace that Michael is overwhelmed. It
makes him feel cheated and angry to
consider the way his wife Elaine would
have brought off the same maneuver.
Worse, Michael realizes it's been years
since his wife bothered with such touches.

"I like the way you do that," he
says.

"This?" Denise says, showing the
two parts of the cylinder and pressing
her lips together to smooth and distrib-
ute the gloss.

Michael nods.

"Really," the woman says. "Don't
you like the way Mrs. Kane does it?"

"What makes you think I'm married?"

"I know all about you, Michael Kane!"
Denise says gaily, returning the lip
gloss to her satchel. As she does, the
mouth of the bag swings wide. Something grey and metallic reflects from
within, catching Michael's eye. At a
quick glance it looks an awful lot like a
pistol.

"Two questions, Denise."

"Yes. One at a time or both together?--or do I have a choice?"

"How and why do you know all about me and what the hell is that in your satchel?"

Denise leans forward a little to look straight into Michael's eyes. Her expression is at once mischievous and mysterious.

"What a pity," she says, throwing her head back to drink deeply from the flask. Michael stares at the way her throat works as the liquid goes down, the delicate things just under the skin like intricate tumblers shifting imperceptively against each other. She lowers the flask and holds it out to him again. "I can't tell you yet how or why I know about you. It will all come out in due time. You will have to be patient, my dear."

"And the gun?" Michael asks.

"Gun? What gun?" Denise is coy.

"In your bag. The grey one." Michael is persistent.

"That's not a gun, silly. That's my vibrator. I never travel without it. You know in case there is no attractive man around when I happen to be in the mood."

Michael is not distracted by her flip talk. He holds out the palm of his hand.

"May I see it? Please?"

"Do you have a search warrant in case I refuse."

Denise is apparently determined to play the scene to its limit.

"No, but I might get violent at any moment. If you know all about me, then you already are aware of my temper. You also know that I am brutally strong. O.K.? May I see it please?"

Denise at first persists in an expression of resistive denial but then a slow smile appears, cooling the confrontation.

"Of course, my dear. Anything you say. But please don't let anyone see it. And don't do anything foolish like pressing the trigger to see if it's loaded."

She reaches into her bag, extracts the weapon and places it in the palm of Michael's outstretched hand. There is a moment of silence as he studiously contemplates the weapon and its possible significance and innuendo.

Michael asks almost in a whisper.

"How did you get this past the inspection station?"

Denise mocks his whisper and responds in kind.

"Oh, I have my ways."

"Why? What is it for?" He persists, still not believing any of this is happening.

Denise laughs softly.

"You silly ass!   A gun is to kill people, of course!"

Michael is stunned, his mouth drops open, his lower lip quivering. His voice struggles in his throat to find some words to say but before Michael can say a word, Denise is up on her feet, leaning in through the seats ahead. "Children," he hears her say, her voice a truly marvelous music, "is everything all right up here?   All comfy and cozy?

Los Angeles Suburb, 1:30 A.M.

The phone on Dr. David Kane's desk jangles for his attention but it will have to wait its turn and due course. The focus of his preoccupation is a manuscript in his hands and he is one of those fortunates endowed with masterful control of his concentration. David simply mentally records the fact that there is a waiting call but then blocks out its disturbing sound until he completes the thought process that absorbs him at the moment.

Now he is ready to speak.

"Hello!   Dr. David Kane here!"

"Good morning, Dr. Kane.   How are you?   This is Walter King from New York."

The voice of David's literary agent is one he is always glad to hear. David had authored several bench mark text books on his research in the field of microbiology. They had achieved great scientific acceptance but, because of their highly specialized field of interest, limited financial success. However he has been bitten by the bug--the writing bug. He knew he wrote well and now he aspired to greater literary recognition. He had always wanted to write fiction-- and why not? Success had come to Dr. David Kane in everything he had ever attempted. The combination of native intelligence and dedication had rewarded him with prestige and recognition.

David wore his success like a naval officer displayed his rank. It was obvious in the confidence of his assured manner. The deeply masculine tones of his vibrant voice would do credit to an evangelist seeking to sway a throng. They were positive and firm but precise in their modulation and moderation. Women particularly were entranced by his boyish handsome face and tall athletic form.

Dr. David Kane was unaccustomed to failure. Success was wooed by him with all the vigor of his being. It was expected--anticipated--not to be denied him.

But now he courts an enigma of an

uncharted variety--a Catch 22 affair. He has a burning desire to write the great American novel--and receive all the plaudits and laurels attendance to that noble feat.   He has written an outline and the first one hundred pages and then sent them on to Walter King for his review. It is a family saga--a reflection of his father, his grandfather, and himself in a fictionalized version depicting the brutality of the times of his Russian ancestors, the inheritance of their American dream and the inter-relationships between fathers and sons.

David Kane thinks of the work as a kind of catharsis--a cleansing of his soul--and what was even more significantly vital to him--perhaps in the struggle of the writing and the telling he could discover what has gone wrong that has led to the real life destruction of his relationship with his father Nathan Kane and his son David Kane.

"How are you, Walter? Nice to hear from you. How is the weather out there?"

David doesn't give a damn about the weather in New York City. He fully expects and awaits the words of approval from Walter King--a man of solid literary perception, reputation, and connection who has found anxious publishers for

David's previous technical manuscripts.

"The usual, Dr. Kane, you know rainy and cold. We could sure use some of that California sunshine."

"Have you had a chance to read the work I've sent you on my new novel "Our Fathers Before Us?""

"Yes, I have, Dr. Kane."

"What do you think?"

"I think you have a rare gift, Dr. Kane, the ability to write complex technical material in a coherent objective manner and then also to possess a literary fictional capability as well."

David's spirits soar with expectation.

"Do you think you can sell it to a big-name publisher, Walter?"

There is a brief pause at the distant end signaling some uncertainty.

"I don't think so, Dr. Kane."

David is momentarily stunned at the words, unaccustomed to negative response and rejection.

His voice works hard, catching in his throat, for once the keen mind untracked by the disappointing answer.

"Wha-a-a-t? What do you mean?"

"There are some facts you have to know, Dr. Kane. The world of fiction is a different league--a different ball game. The competition is intense and there are many factors that come into play here."

"I don't understand. What factors?"

"The publishing business is in a slump and the publishers are protecting their bottom line: the profit margin. They are only going with established name writers whose reputations guarantee a certain sales volume. Gone With The Wind couldn't get printed today if it was by an unknown author."

Anger and resentment well up inside of David but his voice continues calm and firm.

"I see. Although I am a recognized technical author, it counts for nothing in the fiction field. And it's Catch 22 all over again. I can't get published because I don't have a reputation for fiction and I can't get a reputation for fiction because I can't get published."

There is a nervous cough at the New York end of the line.

"I wouldn't have put it so bluntly but I'm afraid you have summed it up quite correctly, Dr. Kane."

Now there is a pause at both ends. David then asks cautiously.

"No way around all this, Walter? No way at all?"

"None that I can think of."

"I'm a very wealthy man. I'm not doing all this for the money. I only want to prove to myself that I can do it--even if I have to buy my way past this odious conspiracy. Does that suggest anything to you, Walter?"

"Let me think about it, Dr. Kane. I'd like to find a way to beat the system myself."

David's spirits rise ever so slightly.

"That's the way, Walter. Think positively!"

"I will, Dr. Kane. There is another purpose to my call. It has to do with your father."

The words "your father" thrown at him unexpectantly chill him like a bucket of cold water.

"My father? Nathan? What could you possibly have to do with my father?"

"I received a message, Dr. Kane, a message from someone who knows I am your agent. Your father is writing a book also--his memoirs, an expose'--not fiction."

"My father? Writing a book? That's ridiculous. At this stage of his life. He hasn't written in years."

"Maybe not. But he has a publisher. Cronin and Keppler."

"You're kidding? How? Why?"

"Because it's sensationalism. He has a story to tell. It will sell books."

"But, Walter, this kind of book is not in his nature."

"Maybe not - but he's doing it, Dr. Kane. He's putting it all on tape. The publishers will get a ghost writer to put it in shape. But there's a problem--and that's where the message comes in."

"Problem? Message?"

"There are certain influential individuals who are frightened by what a once powerful but now possibly senile old man might say. Your father apparently knows where a lot of bodies are buried. These people don't want to be reminded."

"I see, Walter. What can I do about it?"

"I suggest you try to dissuade him--you know--talk him out of it."

"Some chance. It would be like getting a volcano to quit spewing its lava. You can't <u>talk</u> Nathan Kane out of anything--least of all me. I would be the last person in the world who could communicate with him. We are not on the best of terms."

"Dr. Kane, I suggest you try because these people intend to stop him any way they can."

"You mean-- ."

"Yes, his life could be in danger."

"Thanks for calling, Walter. You think about my proposition and I'll see what I can do about my father."

David Kane returns the telephone instrument to its cradle and is surprised
that he is able to identify an emotion he
has not felt in a long time. He is concerned that harm might come to Nathan
Kane! He sits there quietly meditating
and reflecting on the attitudes he has
held on to for so long--perhaps too
long--regarding the complex push-pull
relationships between fathers and sons.
The news of possible violence attacking
his father has penetrated his armor and
made a shambles of the defense he has
mounted to protect the way he thought
he wanted them to be.

His father Nathan had thrust his love
too hard on him and somehow wounded
David. Therefore David had been determined   not   to   do   the   same   with
Michael--so he invented ways to withhold
his feelings from Michael. All of a
sudden in David's mind the entire delicate fabric of family feelings was coming
apart and he didn't know how to handle
his new emotions.

"My father Nathan Kane was and is
one of a kind--He was and is a self-sus-
taining force like a guru or a volcano--
He never has and still does not need
anyone else--He always insisted and
persisted in doing everything for every-
one--He smothered me and I could not

breathe--He wanted me to be like him but I couldn't because I wasn't and he couldn't understand--Michael is like him, not me--He thinks I hate him--I don't-- You have to worship Ceasar from afar-- It isn't my fault."

Should he call his father to warn him of his danger? Should he go to him? Should he call Michael and ask him to go?

A positive response to any of these questions required the initiation of an action that would break down a wall David had carefully erected stone by stone. It would mean opening the door to the extremely personal interplay-- conversation and concern and affection-- that should exist between fathers and sons - no matter what their differences - simply because--well, as everyone knows, "blood should be thicker than water." But hold on, David thought, the fact that his feeling of concern was there, it existed, must mean that the door had always been there. All he had to do was open it and walk through.

Dr. David Kane explodes from his reverie by pounding his desk with the palm of his hand. To no one at all he screams:

"I can't do it! I can't do it!"

Only David Kane really knows what it

is he finds so difficult to do: admit to himself that this man of near perfection has so seriously erred.

Miami Beach, 11:45 A.M.

Goldmesser enters the bedroom ready to hear the next chapter of Nathan Kane's story.   The bed is empty.   The room is empty.   The uninterrupted whiteness of the place, its blank vacancy grotesque, slams Goldmesser like an avalanche of snow.

He shouts.   "Kane!   Where the hell are you?   I'm too old for hide-and-seek!"

The power of Kane's answer, the resonant bass restored to full volume again, is just as startling as his absence from the bed.

"In here!   In the crapper!"

Goldmesser goes toward the voice, and his search carries him through a door to the right and on through two adjoining dressing rooms and then into a marvel of a bathroom, a large open area agleam with the polished surfaces of marble and terrazzo and glass, an array of goldplated fixtures adding special points of brilliance in the glow that filters through the skylight overhead.

Goldmesser whistles in appreciation.

"So this is how the rich make kaka.

You'll agree with me, Mr. Kane, it's a long way from Horka."

Kane's huge frame teeters before one of the two low-profile commodes, his white cotton trousers settled awkwardly at his ankles.

"Shut up," he says, "I'm trying to take a leak, and it's not so easy as it used to be."

"Be my guest," Goldmesser says, wheezing as he seats himself on a kind of platform that curves gracefully along the edge of the sunken tub. "But if you don't mind my saying so, Mr. Kane, do you feel up to running around. Friday left you in my care, you know."

"Enough!" Kane roars. "You and that schvarzer give me a headache with your mothering. Besides, you're too small to carry a bedpan big enough to handle my business."

Goldmesser gives in and laughs a little, and Nathan joins him, the two old men laughing against the background of Kane's dribbling stream. Goldmesser watches as Kane hikes up his trousers and buttons himself and then washes his hands in the fancy sink.

"Come on," Kane says, leading the way, his towering body again suggestive of vast reserves of strength, "I'll get us something to nosh. Time you fed your face, Goldmesser. With luck, it'll keep your mouth shut for a while."

Goldmesser hastens after Kane, his short legs working double-time to keep up with the big man's strides.

"Listen, shtarker," he calls to the broad back advancing ahead of him, "I don't think this is such a hot idea."

In the kitchen, Kane wheels around to face the small man hurrying after him. "What isn't? Life?"

"Now, now, Mr. Kane, please--I'm already worn out with what's happened today. This is already more excitement in a few hours than I've had since the union negotiations and strikes I used to have with you. Remember?"

Kane turns away and busies himself at the refrigerator, pulling things out and kicking the door closed and settling this and that on the long butcher-block counter opposite. He pauses for a moment and reflects almost sentimentally:

"Who could forget those days? They were exciting, they were really something!"

Goldmesser stands in the doorway, his hands on his hips, his heavy eyeglasses canted well down onto his fleshy nose.

"So, Mr. Kane, at this stage of your life you need all this crazy business with

shootings and bombings? Is it worth it?
Why don't you forget this expose you
are writing and let sleeping dogs lie?
Why do you want to make these people
so angry? You have a compulsion to be
carried out in little pieces?"

The old man explodes, his face reddening.

"When I want your two cents worth,
I'll ask for it, Mr. Buttinsky. Til then
butt out! Just because you happened to
come along and give me a ride in your
car--which I wouldn't have taken if I
was conscious--doesn't entitle you to
give me the third degree and psychoana-
lyze my motives. Got it?"

Goldmesser throws up his boney arms
in a gesture of surrender.

"O.K., O.K. I got it! I didn't mean
anything. I just don't want to see anyone get hurt. Friday was lucky."

"It will take more than a bomb to
make a dent in that black army tank.
Where the hell is he already anyway."

"I'm sure he'll be back as soon as he
is patched up."

Goldmesser sighs with the very limits
of human exasperation. He thumbs his
glasses back into position.

"You don't learn a lesson, do you,
Kane? Nothing but the final big bang is
going to teach you. Am I right?"

Kane, no longer angry, pauses in his work at the counter to face the little man. "My friend," he says, his manner returning to exuberance, his face lit up with ruddiness again, his wintry blue eyes blazing with rekindled fire, "for the first time since I've made your acquaintance, I am delighted to say you are one hundred percent right! Now I'm composing a little sandwich here, muenster and mayonnaise on white. Do you want one or not?"

"Sure," Goldmesser nods. "Who gets to eat from a crazy man's hands every day of the week? You're in such a hurry to get killed, go ahead."

"Get killed, don't get killed, meanwhile this is life!" Kane roars.

"Life," Goldmesser echoes, nodding despite himself, helpless in the face of Kane's irresistible energy. But then he sees how this is irresponsible, improper, a mistake--and he moves to play from his strongest suit. "Listen," Goldmesser says, leaning against the doorjamb, "maybe it's time someone leveled with you--because the doctor didn't have time to do it. Aside from anybody getting to kill you, they might be disappointed because you might not live that long. You are not in that great shape."

Nathan doesn't appear to be listening.

He slices the sandwiches in half and goes to get plates.

"Wait a minute," he says, stopping in his search, "where are my cigarettes?"

"I hid them. Besides, you never finished your story."

Nathan Kane stands in the middle of the whitetiled room, his massive arms folded across his chest.

"You're such a silly putz, Goldmesser. Number one, I'm not finishing any story. Number two, I keep an emergency supply right in here."

He is just moving for the utility drawer when the doorbell rings.

"I'll get it," Goldmesser quickly responds.

"Like hell you will!" Nathan shouts. "This is my house!"

He pushes past Goldmesser and heads for the front door, hurrying like a young man and hardly like a man who moments ago was flat on his back, his heart for the moment high with the prospect of who might be there to be greeted, to be hugged, to be kissed. He forgets the possible danger presented by strangers there. He yanks the door open, his heart rejoicing, the name already on his lips.

"Mi--!"

But it is not Michael Kane who is

standing there, but instead an attractive coffee-skinned woman in a starched white uniform. In her hand she has a black medical bag, and she quickly raises the other hand to slap her palm against the door and force back Kane's effort to slam it in her face.

"Out!" Kane shouts. "Definitely out! Watch out for what she's got in that bag!"

But Kane is no match for the woman's agility and determination, and she steps past him into the middle of the room. She sweeps her eyes around, sizing things up, already taking charge of the situation.

"You're the neighbor?" she says to Goldmesser, who stands there shrugging in Kane's direction.

"That's me."

"And he's the nut, right?"

"That's him."

The woman turns her glowering attention on Kane, who still stands by the open door, the knob still in his hand. "Now I want you to know something, mister. My name is Doctor Henderson--I am the assistant to the doctor who treated you after your collapse and one thing I don't do is I don't take no jazz from nobody. Which is why I'm what the doctor ordered--because I am

the doctor--because the way I hear it
you're just jumping with jazz. Now what
the hell you doing out of bed, goddamn-
it!"

Kane's face is alive with rage.

"A black doctor?--a woman yet--too?
What will they think of next? Friday,
where the hell are you?"

He looks from the woman to Goldmesser, as if here is where the accusation
belongs, and then he jerks his attention
back to the woman, who stands implaca-
bly, a monument of stone, beautiful even
in the face of anger in the middle of the
floor.

"Mr. Kane," Goldmesser says, coming
forward a little, "I didn't get a chance
to tell you. This lady doctor is here to
check up on you. Frankly there was
some doubt as to the odds on your sur-
vival. Now if you'll just close the door
and sit down for a minute,--" "Out!"
Kane roars. "The both of you! First
check her bag. She if she has a gun.
She might have been sent by them"

Goldmesser looks hard at Kane.

"You're a lunatic! You really are!"

"Out! This is private property!"

"Mr. Kane," Goldmesser says, spread-
ing his small hands in appeal, "I beg
you, you may be a sick man. She
doesn't want to hurt you. Please,

please cooperate."

"Out, vantz! And take that schvartze with you!"

Goldmesser stares in disbelief.

"Now you listen up, you honky fruit-cake!" It is the black woman, and she is advancing on Kane and shouting as she comes. "This here's a free country, but it ain't so free we let screwballs kill theirselves." The woman plants herself squarely in front of Kane, and she drops her black bag to the floor where she stands. "Now you can holler all you want, but I came here to do a job, and I'm just as hardassed as you any day in the week and a damn sight just as stubborn. So you let go that goddamn door and start moving toward that bed--because what this here man is telling you is true--I'm a doctor and nobody bad sent me to kill you and I ain't going to stand for no shit from you."

Kane stands his ground. He looks around--as if there might be some weapon handy with which to beat back his attackers. If only Friday were here, he would know how to deal with this outrageous Dr. Henderson. But there is only his righteous indignation to draw on. He straightens himself to his full height. He seems to be casting about for a better definition of sovereign territory,

some proof of personal sanctuary as yet
unexplored. But he has nothing to declare save his outrage, and he raises
himself to a thunderous pitch to declare
it.

He bellows in the woman's face, "I
said get ou--!"

But Nathan Kane never finishes the
rounding out of his protest. And when
he collapses, it is the black woman who
catches him, staggering and then going
down with him under the old man's great
falling weight.

Delta 84, 12:00 A.M.
The Boeing 727 holds to a steady course
due south now, the three titanic engines
at tail and wings geared down to cruising power. Outside, where the air is
clear and the sky above is hard blue,
the temperature is forty-seven degrees
below zero, but inside, in the first-class
cabin, there is nothing but comfort, low
noise, and the even glide of the aircraft's steely vector through time and
space.

The flight attendants move through
the aft cabin now, inching a cart along
the aisle as they serve cocktails and
carbonated drinks and canapes to the
handful of passengers who occupy seats
up here. When the cart comes to the

two children who sit to the front of her, Denise motions to a stewardess and requests milk. The children protest, plead a bit for Coke or any kind of soda, but their resistance is mild, and the woman stifles it with no more than a look and a word.

For herself, Denise asks for a Tab, patting her flat stomach by way of explanation. When the stewardess smiles questioningly at Michael, he does not answer right away but turns instead to Denise.

"What was that in the flask? Maybe they've got some more of it."

"Southern Comfort?" She says as the stewardess reaches in to adjust the tray before her. "Not likely, darling, not likely."

"Yeah, I guess not," Kane says. "I'll have a Tab also," he says to the stewardess and then he adds "No thanks" when the stewardess offers the tray of canapes.

They drink in silence for a moment, Michael and Denise. The gun has been returned to her bag, its reason for being unclear and Denise still unwilling to add clarification or explanation. Michael tries desperately to reconstruct the events of the brief encounter time with Denise, seeking some logical pur-

pose to this delightful though frustrat-
ingly bizarre experience.   But it's no
use his trying to think a thought for
long in Denise's company.   Michael can
not make much headway against the
interference the woman's sensuality im-
poses, and given that sensuality's residence in a woman who is also intent on
appearing totally mysterious or capri-
cious or dangerous, and who may in fact
be all these things, Michael can't do
much more than simply listen for what's
coming next.   Perhaps, he thinks, the
best approach is a very direct one--
confront her--come to grips with whatever motivates this strange behavior.

Should he? he asks himself.

It is a question he needn't have
bothered with.   Denise holds Michael
Kane in a grip he could not break if he
tried.   And he is willing to understand
he does not want to try.   But he is also
willing to understand that her fascination
for him is not strictly a matter of the
promise of her body, of some unimaginable passion that might be realized when
Delta 84 sets down.   It is something else
in this woman that seizes Michael and
holds him in readiness for the playing
out of her games.   It is something
vaguely to do with last chances, the
possibility of release, the prospect of

some cure for whatever it is that has made his life the lifeless thing it is. Yesterday, before he had ever met Denise, Michael had been quietly nursing the sorrow of his unsatisfactory marriage to Elaine and quickly stewing it in brandy. He had again been visited by the desperate feeling that has always captured him whenever he's felt himself utterly abandoned, entirely alone.

Now suddenly from seemingly no-where, there was Denise and all the attributes that composed her, some utterly irresistible--others painfully unfathomable. And after that there was this sudden madness with his beloved grandfather, Nat, who in his antiquity decides to be a tell-all author. Michael had almost forgotten Nat was his sole reason for being here at all--soaring through space toward Miami in an alumi-num gondola--to try to dissuade his grandfather from his dangerous project in order to save his life. He knew he must get the old man's face in front of him and get the whole thing out--what Nat knows, what only Nat can tell--and then persuade him to forget it. But now that urgency doesn't seem so pressing--and maybe it was a damn fool idea in the first place. Maybe no man can change another--and God knows--Nathan Kane was no ordinary man. Nat must have his good reasons for what he is doing! But Michael sure had to find out what they are.

"Well?" Denise says.

"Well what?" Michael says, shifting in his seat and basking in her loveliness.

"So why are you going to Miami, Michael Kane?"

"I have the strange feeling you already know."

"Indulge me, darling. Tell me anyhow."

Michael decides to try for some reciprocity.

"If I tell you, will you tell me why you are?"

"Oh, you want to play "Show and Tell?" Haven't we already shown each other everything we have?" Denise asks with a feigned look of virginal innocence.

"I have--but you, my dear Denise, have yet to let me see all your cards. When are you going to level with me--before my mind runs away with all the unimaginables?"

"We will see, darling. You will have to trust me."

"How's about no more fencing, right?" Michael asks. "What do you say to total and absolute honesty, right?"

Denise looks away from him for a moment as if stalling for time for thought. She turns back to him.

"Again," she says "you will have to trust me. You do trust me, Michael, don't you? I haven't disappointed you so far, have I? So why are you going to Miami?"

Michael has to admit that their relationship thus far has been many things--but not disappointing. Besides, he reasons, she probably knows the whole story anyway. So from the beginning Michael recounts his life's story, the strange relationship with his father David, the closeness with his grandfather and now the sudden compulsion of Nathan Kane to publish his candid memoirs and the great danger entailed therein. He tells Denise he is on an urgent mission to keep the old man from harm. When he has finished, Michael gives Denise that "Now it's your turn" expectant look.

It is not immediately forthcoming--but she is talking.

"My, my, Michael. You certainly do have some problems. Things should certainly have been more settled by this stage of your life. All your advantages--the grandson of the notorious

Nathan Kane, the son of the illustrious Dr. David Kane--a national labor leader in your background, and an internationally-celebrated biochemist for a father--my, my--and you, Michael Kane, you yourself an important attorney, it is so unfortunate you can't get your family to just love one another. What on earth do you think is the heart of the problem the men in your family seem to have?"

Michael is aware that Denise is taking an attack course in conversation to avoid being put on the defensive herself--but he feels he must respond to this.

"We all have too much love inside us and we have difficulty in channeling it and displaying it properly. We also have a tendency to love too well--but not too wisely. And now for you, sweet Denise, What is it with you? Why are you going to Miami?"

They are face to face with one another, her lovely lips barely six inches from his. An impish grin appears, her eyes darting from left to right and then back again.

"The answer is really quite simple," she says. "I'm just taking my children to see their grandfather!"

The response asks more questions than it answers for Michael--not knowing what to make of it.

With that statement Denise gets up
and pushes past him, her legs making no
effort to avoid a pleasurable contact.
The proximity is too much for Michael.
He puts his hands to her hips to help
her get by, and he leaves his hands
there and works his fingers into her
flesh before she's made it into the aisle.

"Children," she says. "I'm just going to the lavatory for a minute, in case
you turn around and don't see me.   I'll
be back in a jiff, okay?"

Michael wrenches around in his seat
to watch Denise's stately retreat toward
the rear of the plane, and then he comes
forward again, his body alive with sensation.

"I want her," he mutters to himself.
"My God, do I want her."   The thought
beclouds all his reason, rendering him
once more incapable of logical analysis.
When Denise returns she has somehow
managed to change her outfit to a very
summery one: a thin red halter top that
barely contains her abundant assets and
a pair of tight white shorts.   Michael
does not help her get by him this time.
He does not reach his hands to Denise's
waist to help her ease past him to her
seat.   But as if she is deciphering
Michael's very thought and hesitation
and is shifting her strategy in accord

with his retreats, she twists and struggles more than seems necessary, an excess of awkwardness that somehow brings one of her hands twice into contact with his upper thigh and also a breast into grazing proximity with his face. The air once more hums with the lavender fragrance that surrounds her, the odor so pungent that the renewed effect on Michael is again Oriental, as if he has suddenly stepped back into an exotic temple where cunningly concealed pots of smouldering incense cloud the ethers and the brain.

"Darling," Denise says, as she fits her buttocks into the seat, her voice glittering with blithe spirit, "tell me, did you miss me awfully?" She gives her hair a quick gay toss, her lips drawn back in a broad smile to show the glinting whiteness of her teeth.

The woman seems in the very best of moods, undaunted and unrelenting in the role she is playing or its affect on Michael. Things seem to be progressing very nicely per her script and her schedule. "Look," Michael says, "before we have any more of this, let's just get a few things straight."

"But Michael, precious," Denise says, "whatever is the matter? You're not objecting to my new outfit, are you?"

She looks at him, her eyes wide with mock innocence. "I rather like it my-self--especially for the hot weather that is definitely ahead."

"Now wait a minute," Michael says, turned in his seat so that he faces her. He puts his hand to her knee and grips it. "It's lines like that."

"Like <u>what</u>, pray tell?" Denise ex-claims, her expression seeming one of earnest concern.

"<u>You</u> know," Michael says, trying to steady himself. "Things that almost seem to be saying two things."

"But of course, Michael," she says. "Isn't that what happens when one is playing the usual game. The future is yet to be seen. You must have pa-tience, my sweet."

"You're confusing me," Michael stam-mers. "You know that's what you're do-ing and you're <u>doing</u> it: the gun, your being on this very plane. You're driv-ing me nuts!"

"Am I?" sings cheerily. "Well, it will all stop in due time."

Michael reaches for a cigarette, and Denise quickly takes up the heavy light-er and lights it for him.

"This is really very handsome," she says, rubbing her thumb back and forth across the brass. "Was it a gift,

Michael?"

"My grandfather--" He begins.

"Something Nathan gave you? How splendid!"

"Now that's enough," Michael says, squeezing her knee. "Stop it now. I'm asking you to stop it. Just cut it out and tell me how the hell you know my father's name and even my grandfather's name. You hear me? I want to know how come you know all about us."

The woman looks down to the lighter, to the continuing action of her slender tapering thumb going back and forth against the brass. "Oh, Michael," she says, "now don't you see how it's you that's getting me all confused? One minute you want to know about a gun and the next minute you can't wait to know about a name, and, honestly, I just don't know what you really want to know about from one minute to the next."

"Those kids," Kane says, jerking his head toward the seatbacks in front. "They're Kesslers, and you're Steiner. Explain that, just to begin with, okay?"

"Is that troubling you too? Oh, Michael, is there no end to what unnerves you? You persist in trying to obliterate all potentiality between us with these absurdly trifling questions. Denise finishes her speech and casts her

eyes up into his. "We are two attractive
and intelligent adults, Michael Kane. Do
you agree with me so far?"

Michael is held by her eyes, by the
surpassing beauty of her face. He sees
again that it is that face, that special
face, the one that prefigures all the
rest. He can't help himself. He grins.
"Yes," he says, his voice hoarse. "Of
course."

"Now then," the woman says, smiling,
eyes searching Michael's, "it is also
evident that we want each other. Do we
continue to agree?"

Michael feels himself losing his purchase on the seat. He feels as if he is
about to reel forward.

"Yes. Yes, of course," he is able to
say.

"Look down," he hears her saying.
"Down here where my thumb touches this
surface. Do you see?"

Slowly, as if his neck will snap like a
stick if the movement is faster, Michael
lowers his gaze.

"See my thumb go to and fro. See
how steady the motion is, the pressure
firm enough but light enough. Back and
forth, back and forth, ever so lightly
but felt, felt."

Michael stares, frozen, his ears flooding with the woman's soft, drifting re-

citation, his eyes gazing fixedly at the oscillating thumb, the brass gleaming in the sunlight.

"Oh, Michael, Michael Kane," he hears her say, "everything, simply everything, will be explained, and even then I doubt that you will believe. Look at my thumb. Listen, darling, and watch. Consider the penis in a condition of maximum erection, the shaft arched upward, the glands trembling, the frenulum exposed. See my thumb, it glides to and fro, firmly, yet lightly. It would be moistened perhaps, perhaps with some cream or some jellied substance or with my saliva if you prefer. Just here. On that ring of exquisite sensation. To and fro. My thumb. Do you understand? When we land. This afternoon. This evening. All through the night. Firmly. Yet lightly. Feelings you never thought possible. To and fro, back and forth, over and over. Everything happening. Happening truly, and openly, and utterly. You see what I'm saying, don't you? Do you understand what I am saying?"

Kane can scarcely summon his voice, and when it comes to him, it is a breathy, limpid sound. "Yes," he whispers, and falls silent again, waiting for Denise to say more, wanting nothing but the shimmering spell her images drape over him. Never before has he felt himself so alive to someone and so fused to the moment and so emptied of everything save of what his senses are rushing to his brain.

Forgotten for the moment is the urgent purpose of his mission to his grandfather and his suspicions as to the real and true nature of this remarkable enigmatic woman and her gun. Is she a "hit-man" or a sophisticated "for hire" lady drawn into a unique web of circumstances with her children? She has induced a near hypnotic spell in him that has sealed off all other knowledge or sight but the enchantment of her voice and face.

"It goes on and on like this, like my thumb, back and forth, a slow, steady, incessant ticking, firmly yet lightly until we both cannot bear any more and we explode, and together we soar from ourselves and then fall, Michael, mindlessly spiraling down. Until morning."

She looks up at him.

"Here, Michael. Look at me. You understand? Until morning. Because when morning comes, we will all know the truth and have to face its reality. You may like it or you may not. We will see. You understand me?"

"I think so," Kane says, his vision clearing.

"But before the truth and what it might reveal, we will have our night so if nothing else we will have that to remember. A fling. But it will be a night that will live with you forever. Whether there will be many more nights depends."

"On what?" Michael says.

"On how everyone involved is able to handle the truth, my dear."

"But the children," Kane says. "And how you know so much about me and my family. Tell me, Denise. I want to know."

The woman moves her face close to his, and then she comes closer still, until her lips are almost touching his. "Later," she says. "I promise you. It's all part of the truth. When it's time, Michael, I will tell you. It's really very simple. Really it is. We all have to do--well--what we have to do. Michael Kane--but when you are told how I know such a great deal about you, you will know that in a curious way, it was or- dained. But first I want your word that we will go from the airport directly to my hotel. Do I have your word?" the woman says, her large eyes opened wide with expectation.

"Of course," Michael whispers. "Of course. Denise--I want you,--I want you so very, very much."

The woman brushes her lips against his, and on the instant Michael is overcome by a dizzying pulse of feeling. He starts to seize her, but she moves herself back into her seat and faces primly forward.

"Later, darling, later," she whispers. Then she faces forward again. "Shouldn't they be serving by now?"

Michael again has to shift his gears due to her subtle misdirection. He glances at his watch. "It's about a two-and-a half hour flight," he says. "Yeah, I guess we're past due for eats, all right. You hungry?"

"Not really. But the children," Denise says, looking around for the flight attendants.

Kane looks too.

"Right on the button," he says, when he sees a stewardess coming up the aisle with menus in her hand and distributing them to the few passengers that have seats in first-class. "I guess we're running a little late," he says, facing around and checking his watch again.

"Is anyone meeting you?" Denise says, bending over to lift her carry-all from the floor and into her lap.

"Sometimes there's a car for me. But not this time. I couldn't reach my grandfather to tell him."

"He isn't expecting you?" Denise says.

"Oh, I think he is," Michael says.

"How about you? The children's grandfather is expecting you?"

"No, not really. It's going to be a big surprise."

"Any special occasion?" he asks.

"Very special. You can come along if you like. Would you?" Denise asks.

Michael fairly leaps at the opportunity, recognizing it as the first faint opening of her mysterious door.

"I would love too," he responds.

"Good, then, it's settled. First thing tomorrow morning," Denise says with finality.

Michael thinks for a moment.

"How's about this, Denise? I have to get up to my grandfather's tomorrow too--as early as I can. Suppose the four of us--you know you, me, and the children go to their grandfather and then we all go to see mine?"

"Together? Like a family group?" she asks.

"Yeah--I guess so."

"That would be nice. O.K." Denise says.

Michael reflects for a moment on the inference of what has just happened here. In one brief moment he has been propelled symbolically into a husband and father figure-head position having Denise for a wife and her children as his. He smiles as he finds he likes the idea very much. Yet it does not yet dispel all his doubts about her--the gun etal.

Denise rummages through her carry-all, bringing a paperback book out and then dropping the large leather satchel back onto the floor.

She holds the paperback book in her lap, her hands clasped and resting on the cover. It is not until the stewardess offers Michael the menus for both seats and he passes one over to Denise and she lifts one hand to take it and then the other hand to open it that Michael sees the cover of the book. What he sees sends a bolt of current flashing along his back.

The type is large and very plain, red and blue lettering on a glossy white cover. The title is not a popular one, but it is famous enough.

The Breaking of the Genetic Code.

As for the author's name, it too is famous in certain circles, although not very widely known. Yet among scientists of a particular pursuit, the name is a thoroughly familiar one. But to Michael Kane, the name is as well known as his own, the letters shouting out from the glossy cover, yielding a perfect symmetry, a balance as unchallengeable as that of the man whose name it is.

Dr. David Kane.

The woman studies her menu. She gives the appearance of being totally absorbed by it. But then, without looking at Michael, without taking her eyes from the choices of foods listed, without the least expression in her voice, Denise says, "It's an interesting text. Many people are reading it."

Miami Beach, 12:30 P.M.

She touches behind an ear, and then lower down, on the neck, her strong brown fingers palpating the weathered flesh for a pulse. She puts her head to his chest, listening for a time, and then she leans back on her heels and raises one lid and then the other, peering into Kane's eyes as if the climate of the interior of the skull might be viewed and thus assessed. She lifts one leg at the knee and lets it fall, and then she repeats the test with the other leg. She works each arm in a similar fashion, and

then she puts her fingers to his neck
again and follows the sweep of the
second hand on her wristwatch for the
completion of a circle, her lips pressed
together, her breath whistling through
her nose.

"So?" Goldmesser says when the woman takes her fingers away from Kane's
neck and reaches in back of her to remove some things from the black bag.

"Just hold on now," Dr. Henderson
says, wrapping the grey length of air-
celled fabric around Kane's arm and
raising the earpieces of the stethoscope
into listening position. She squeezes the
rubber bulb and watches as the column
of mercury jumps to increasing levels of
altitude until it reaches one that is high
enough, and then she releases the valve
so that the pressure slowly dissipates
with a hiss and a reading of high and
low can be made. She repeats the pro-
cedure to confirm values, and then she
puts everything away and makes a few
notations on the pad she takes from her
pocket.

She looks up at the small man who
squats to the other side of the massive
prostrate form, his soft round face knot-
ted with tension and the first small concessions to real grief.

"Hey now," Dr. Henderson says,

"there ain't no call to get yourself in a state. This here old buzzard's too damn mean to give us the pleasure." The tall coffee-colored woman stands, getting up in gradual stages of ascent. She looks down at Kane and Goldmesser, who still squats alongside the body, his spectacles in his hand, his eyes squeezed shut. "He's just fainted, is all," the woman says, putting out her hand to help Goldmesser up. "Come on, now," she says, stepping around Kane and tapping Goldmesser's shoulder. "Up we go."

She gets Goldmesser standing and then she goes back to her bag to remove something else, which she quickly cracks between her fingers and then, bending to Kane again, waves back and forth under his nose, her other hand reaching in under his head to lift it slightly. Kane jerks his head from side to side to escape whatever it is the woman holds pinched between her fingers, and then the old man gags a little and coughs and shouts, "Genug! Genug!"

"When you speak English!" Dr. Henderson shouts back, still chasing his nostrils with her pinched fingers, but then lowering Kane's head to the deep white carpet when his eyes open and he sees her and quietly says: "Enough."

The woman stays crouched over Kane,

studying his color, his reactions.

"You want to tell me how you feel?" she says.

"No!" Kane shouts.

"I must be pretty dumb to ask. Here," she says, "I'll give you an easy one--you have any liquor in this place?"

"You want to steal something," Kane answers, "then steal my watch. I don't want to be responsible for drunken schvartzes prowling the streets."

The woman smiles. "Lord God, but you are a sassy one." She stands up. She looks at Goldmesser, who's fiddling with his eyeglasses--putting them on, getting them in place, and then taking them off. "Don't you go worrying about this old goat, Mr..."

"Goldmesser. A neighbor."

"Yeah. Pleased to meet you. Anyway, he ain't going nowhere until he gets good and ready, and that won't be until he's wore out all his mustard. And you can see how that ain't going to be never." She looks down at Kane, who looks back up at her, grinning. "Where's your booze, you sonofabitch? Because I'm just about finished messing with you."

"Get me up and I'll confess."

"Now ain't that sweet," Dr. Henderson says, motioning to Goldmesser to help her get the old man to his feet.

"In the freezer." Nathan Kane says when he is standing again, and Goldmesser goes quickly to the kitchen, returning with a glass and a bottle of Schlichte.

"Go get another one," Dr. Henderson orders, and as Goldmesser goes back for another glass, she takes Kane by the elbow and moves him toward the bedroom.

"No," Kane says. "Where the hell is that damned Friday?"

Dr. Henderson laughs.

"Friday? Oh my, now I recognize you. You're Robinson Crusoe, aren't you? Who is Friday?"

"He's one of yours. I mean he's much blacker than you are but he's white on the inside."

The tawney Dr. Henderson pulls her statuesque body up to her full height and places her hands on her hips in a gesture of outrage.

"Now just what the hell does that mean? And you better have a very good answer or I must just help you along to succumb right here and now!"

"See!" Nathan points at her as he shouts. "I told you to search her. She's one of them. She's out to do me in!"

"The only one who is doing you in is yourself. Now don't evade the issue and explain those remarks about this here Friday person!"

The old man is obviously tiring and wants no more of this high-tension dialogue.

"O.K., o.k." Nathan says. "His real name is Dearheart Hoskins. I've arranged to support him ever since he was a baby. His father got killed saving my life in a garment district labor riot. I've sent him to college and taken care of his mother. He thinks of me as his father. He was a great pro football player til he got kicked in the head. He's been my manservant and friend ever since. Any questions?"

Nathan's explanation calms Dr. Henderson's mood.

"And this business about doing you in and searching me?" she says.

Patiently Nathan explains about the book he is taping and the furor it is raising.

"O.K. come on to bed. You afraid to lie down, old man?"

Kane pulls his arm away from her.

"I'll lie down on the couch," he says, slowly making his way across the carpet in another direction as Goldmesser comes back into the livingroom. He sets the bottle and the glasses down on the coffee table, the harsh white surface empty of everything save the two bronze boys and the five volumes of books held upright between them, four the works of Dr. David Kane and one--On the Picket Line--the early memoirs of a more widely known figure, a former recognized force in the American labor movement, David Kane's father, Nathan Kane.

Goldmesser pours the clear liquid into the two glasses, first offering one to the striking looking Dr. Henderson, who shakes her head. "No," she says, "that's for you. For Hopalong Cassidy here and for you, because you right now don't look like it would harm you none." She takes the other glass from the coffee table and hunches down alongside the couch.

"Sit up a bit," she says to Nathan Kane, holding the glass for him. "Just a taste, hear?"

But he takes the glass from her, tilts it up, and swallows greedily until Dr. Henderson pulls it away from him and sets it back on the coffee table, and then sits herself down beside the glass to face Nathan, legs spraddled, her body pushed forward, her elbows propped on her shapely thighs.

"Better?"

"None of your bee's-wax."

"There I go asking dumb questions again," the woman sighs. Goldmesser has taken up his vigil to the rear of Kane's vision.

Nathan Kane is reclining now, his fingers knitted behind his head in a posture of boyish nonchalance. "And what the hell kind of doctor are you, anyway?

"The kind that don't take an old fraud like you serious," Dr. Henderson flatly replies, and she seems about to add more when Goldmesser comes away from the head of the couch to place himself in Kane's line of vision.

"My friend," Goldmesser begins. "Dr. Henderson and I are here to help you. Because whether you like it or not, you may be a very sick man and you need close supervision. You may not get to finish this book you are writing unless you behave yourself."

The old man has a distinct twinkle in his eye, as if he has hold of a secret no one else knows.

"If they don't kill me first--"

"Maybe you ought to forget it, eh, Mr. Kane?" Goldmesser volunteers.

Nathan Kane laughs.

"I don't intend to finish it--the book--I don't intend to finish it!"

"What?" Goldmesser is shocked for the moment and then he remembers. "Oh, my God! I forgot to tell you. Your publisher called while you were--eh--cat-napping. He wants you to call him--and Mr. Kane--that's good that you don't intend to finish it. But shouldn't you let somebody know--so they'll stop try-ing to kill you?"

"No!" Nathan thunders. "Don't say a word to anybody. It's a secret. As for my publisher, let him stew for a while. Meanwhile we'll see what happens."

"Happens? What can happen?" Gold-messer is puzzled.

"Whether somebody kills me or any-body comes to my rescue." The old man winks as he speaks.

Goldmesser cannot fathom any of this but still persists in a point he wishes to make: "Now a moment ago, when you were having your little difference of opinion with Dr. Henderson here, I was preparing to tell you something somebody had better te--"

"That reminds me," Nathan Kane interrupts. "One, I don't want her here. Two, I don't want you here. And three, if you're staying, shut up!"

"No, Mr. Kane," Goldmesser says, "I don't really think you want us to go and I will not shut up. You are certainly

entitled to kill yourself--or have somebody kill you--if that's your choice. By
me, that's your inalienable right. But
meanwhile it is my right to behave like a
reasonable, reliable human being who has
no intention of standing around while
another human being is suffering and is
too stiff-necked to cry out. You can't
fool me so fast, my friend, and I'm not
sure you have the strength to fool anybody anymore. Ox? Mr. Kane, don't
kid yourself. Not now. Not anymore.
You're old and you're just like everybody else now, only maybe a little bit
more so. It's time you quit the ox act
and gave yourself a rest."

Kane takes his hands away from behind his head and folds his arms across
his chest. "Scab!" he shouts.

"Maybe so," Goldmesser admits, "but
at least I know when to turn it off,
when to talk up and talk sense. Now
you have indicated that you are expecting your grandson to show up, so we're
all standing around here like numbskulls
waiting for him to do so--but just so I
can rest easy and have a little peace of
mind that I've done my best, I'm going
to ask you one question, and I believe
you owe me an answer. I've done you a
few favors, and the way I see it, you
owe me."

"Two hundred fifty something. Your money you'll get! Just get me my checkbook!"

Goldmesser waves his hand in front of his face as if shooing away flies. "The doctor said you have a son in California. I want his telephone number."

Nathan Kane laughs. "My son? He never told me--I never asked."

"Then I want to know his name and where he lives."

"What for?"

"What for?" Goldmesser says, folding his arms in imitation of Kane. "So I can get him ready to view the remains! That's what for!"

"What remains? Besides he's not interested!"

"Hell," Dr. Henderson says, "I bet he'd come with bells on. I bet he'd pay top dollar for a seat down front."

Nathan snorts, and then he breaks into a fit of coughing. He raises himself on one elbow to catch his breath, and with his other hand he pushes Dr. Henderson away when she moves to help him.

"His name?" Goldmesser insists.

"His name," Nathan repeats with irony. "All right, so his name is David and so he lives in Pasadena--so go call him on the telephone if that'll shut you up and get you out of here."

"That's just what I intend to do," Goldmesser answers, this time with irony of his own. He turns on his heel and goes to the phone, but before he has the receiver in his hand, Kane is back up on his elbow and shouting: "Don't! I was just kidding. I forbid it! Goldmesser, do you hear me? You do not have my permission to do this!"

Goldmesser dials for the operator.

He looks back at Nathan Kane.

"I don't need it," the small man calmly announces, his manner all perfect mildness once more.

"That's right," Dr. Henderson says, holding the glass of whiskey out to Kane again. "This here's a free country, Mr. Charlie."

"Free?" Kane says, staring hard at the woman as he takes the glass from her. "Nothing's free--not countries or people or anything!"

"Well now," the woman says, unperturbed, honestly amused by Kane, "That's the first intelligent thing I've heard get clear of that nasty mouth of yours since I came in here." She puts her hand to the bottom of the glass to help Kane angle it to his lips. And then she puts her face close to Kane's--and in a voice too low for Goldmesser to hear, the woman says: "He's doing what somebody's got to. You hear me, old man? Now drink this booze and be nice and maybe you'll live to get a little more nookie."

Kane takes the rest of the liquor down and the woman removes the glass.

"That may be the best offer I've had in a long time," Kane says, and almost smiles.

The handsome brown woman in starched white recoils in mock offense.

"That wasn't an offer, old man. It was only a maybe." Now I think it might be a good idea to give you another kind of shot to make you feel better. You know--a needle in your ancient white ass."

With that she reaches into her black bag and prepares a hyperdermic needle.

The sound of the front door opening without the announcement of knocking or bell ringing freezes everyone in position. It is Friday who has let himself in with his key. The gleaming white bandage on his forehead wound contrasts with his black skin.

"What the hell is going on here?" he shouts as he confronts Dr. Henderson poised with needle in hand about to inject the old man's peeking buttock.

Goldmesser   vainly   attempts   an

explanation.

"You see--she's a doc--"

Before he can finish, Friday has leaped through the air, twisted the hyperdermic free of Dr. Henderson's hand to send it flying and shattering against the far wall, and pinned the woman in his massive grasp rendering her helpless. A scream of both terror and anger emanates from her frightened wide spread lips and resonates through- out the massive rooms of the apartment. Nathan Kane lies where he is, seemingly amused by the dramatic byplay.

"Let me go, you dumb black bas- tard!" Dr. Henderson shouts as she struggles vainly in Friday's bearhug grasp.

"Not so fast, my pretty," Friday answers calmly without releasing her. "--til I check out just what you are up to here."

Nathan Kane speaks up. "She says she's a doctor. She was about to give me a shot to make me feel better."

"Maybe!" Friday responds.

"Just maybe--or to make you feel nothing at all! You know this guy I dismantled downstairs who brought you the bomb for a present? Right now he and his bomb are sleeping quietly with the fishes out there in the ocean. But

before he went I persuaded him to talk--
to tell me what he knew."

"So what did he tell you?   Nathan
asks anxiously.

Friday tightens his grip on the very
distressed and struggling brown woman
in white.

"He told me that there was a back-up
female "hit-man" sent to do the job on
you in case he failed!"

Delta 84, 12:45 P.M.
"No," Michael says, looking up at the
stewardess who waits to hear his lunch-
eon selection, "nothing for me, thanks."

He sits back and lights a cigarette
while Denise gives the stewardess her
order and also what she wants the children served.

"you should eat something," she
says to Michael.   "I want you brimming
with energy tonight."

"Do you?"   He says with more than a
little sarcasm.   He takes up the paperback from Denise's lap.   He flips the
book over to look at the photograph of
the remarkably attractive man on the
back, pipe jutting from the even teeth,
the smile relaxed, generous, two fingers
of one hand pushing professorially at the
temple, the effect one of genial affability
fused with profound thought.   "He's not

like that," Michael says, tapping the picture of the author.

"No? He looks rather nice, don't you think?"

"Nice?" Michael says. "You'd have to ask one of his lab technicians. They'd know better than I would."

"Really," Denise says, returning the book to her own lap. "Well, one can hardly trust a photograph, of course."

"Oh, come on now," Kane says angrily. "I want to know how you figure in this. What's the Kane family to you, Denise Steiner? How come you know all about us? Have we ever met before? Maybe you had a wig on or something."

"No, Michael," the woman says mildly, her manner still pleasant. "But I've seen pictures of you."

"You have? How?" Michael says. "How come you've seen pictures of me?" He says less irritably now that he seems to be getting somewhere.

"You're well known in theatre, in film."

"I'm no actor," Michael says. "I'm just a producer and sometimes a director. My picture isn't plastered all over the place."

"Oh, well," Denise says, "you're too modest. It seems to me you're often showing up in columns, magazines--the trade papers."

"Wait a minute," Michael says. "Are you from New York?"

Denise smiles. The effect is dazzling, glorious, and for an instant Michael regrets all this, his risking the loss of her favors.

"Look," he says. "I'm sorry, but I've got to get this straight. You're making me so uneasy, Denise. I can't explain it. It gives me the creeps to have you sitting there, so desirable, so maddeningly desirable, and yet at the same time so sort of--I don't know--unsettling. You know things about me. It's strange. And the way we met. And all those odd things you've been doing and saying, as if you're bent on playing with me in some kind of crazy way. Hey, look," Michael says, "you're catching me at a bad time in my life. Maybe that's part of it. Maybe it's me--maybe I'm just reacting crazily to everything that's around me. My wife--" Kane begins, and stops to collect himself. "You see, I'm going through a heavy number--a lousy divorce. I had to drop everything to run down to Miami to see if my grandfather is all right and try to talk him out of this big expose' he is writing. Forget it. The thing is, I'm agitated with my wife and anxious about Nate and you've got me a little crazy--I'm boring you. Am I boring you? You don't bore me. Oh no, Denise Steiner, that's one thing you sure as hell don't do. Hey, come on, this is lousy for me. I don't know how to get this out right. But the point is, everything's happening at once here. My life seems to be at a cross-roads ever since I met you. I mean, last night--with you--well, it was just fantastic for me--and I really thought it was fantastic for you. But today, just being on the same plane with you--that's weird. You're the same--yet you're different--and you carry a gun--and you know all about me and my family. Am I making any sense? You know why I'm on this plane? Because there's only one person in the world besides my mother that really matters to me. You know him--you know his name. My grandfather. Nat. I'm going to him because he needs me. His life might be in danger. Nat's the best. The man's--well, he just goddamn incredible. And there's this thing between us--a bond, a bond that's-- Anyway, the point is I got that call while I was with you that some important people that Nat used to know were frightened by what he might say and didn't want him to say it. They might hurt him--so I'm going down to see if I can talk him out of it--Hey, listen to me, I'm really running off at the mouth. But the trouble is, if I can't convince him, who else can? He's a very stubborn man."

"There's your father," the woman says, and Michael can hear it, that tincture of irony subtly defused through the words.

"My father?"

"He's an intelligent man. Some people insist he's a genius. His opinion is highly respected--and he is your grandfather's son. Wouldn't he be able to influence your father? Why don't you contact him and ask him to?" Denise lowers the tray from the seatback in front of her. She places the paperback off to one side and takes the tray of food the stewardess holds out to her. "You see, Michael, you never gave me a chance to answer you awhile ago. Actually, no, I'm not from New York. My home is in California--and in California one hears a great deal about Dr. David Kane. After all, he's a celebrity--and every so often he appears on television. He seems--so wise. Don't you think he'd want you to confer with him? Wouldn't he want to help in this kind of crisis? The man's your father, after all."

"The man's nothing," Michael says, running his fingers back through his hair. "He's nothing to me. Not since I was a kid has he ever been a father to me--nor a son to his father. Anyhow, we're different--fundamentally different. He's cold. All inside himself. All reason and logic. We're just alien to each other, and that's the long and the short of it. And as for this thing we are in now, he'd just see it as the logical playing out of an inferior personality. That's how he thinks--rational scenarios, but the actors are abstractions, not people. For him, life is a thing you study, not live. He couldn't care less whether his father was in danger or not. But Nat--Nat's all gusto, the great human adventure. I tell you, the man is--well, he's a character, I guess, but he's real. He's done things--from nothing, from starting in the mud--and the sonofabitch has done it with his own two hands. Look," Michael says, "I'll tell you something, and it's crazy, but it's interesting. It was the same way between my grandfather and his dad as it is between me and mine. Just opposites--and no way to reach across the distance. It's just the hard fact of how it's been going in my family from generation to generation. You know, I never really realized this before. I mean, that pattern. Among these four--" Michael starts, but he does not finish his thought--because another thought suddenly snatches at him, something else he's never realized before. He looks down at his hands and then into the aisle, as if something foul has just been spilled onto the floor. He looks back at the woman. He watches her eating. Has she been listening to all this?

"I wonder," Kane says. "If that's the way it will be if I ever have any sons. It just never occurred to me before."

"I don't believe in patterns and as for your father--" Denise says, and daintily forks a bit of food into her mouth. Michael watches her chew, the sweet invention of the small muscles of her face.

"Yeah?" Michael says, thinking, feeling something awful stirring in him.

"Say that again," he says.

"Just that your father really is cold. Perhaps you should consider that. In other words, it may not be a pattern but simply the random toss of the genetic coin. Do you follow me, Michael?"

"I follow you," he says. "But you

said something else too. You said he really is cold. How the hell would you know that?"

Denise Steiner puts down her knife and fork. She turns to face him.

"Oh, that's easy," she says. "But perhaps you'd like to guess."

"Guess?" Michael says. "Give me something to go on."

"Well, let's see," Denise says, and takes up her knife and fork again. She cuts at her meat, lifts the food to her mouth, but holds it there, poised. She turns to Michael, frowning as if in deep thought, her lovely lips pursing, a soft hum sounding from far back in her throat. "Oh, sweet, innocent Michael," the woman says after a time, "there's so much, I scarcely know where to begin."

"Quit playing with me," he snaps, unwilling to take much more of this.

"Really, I'm not," Denise says. "It's just that some things are better revealed to one gradually."

"Yeah, well, don't worry about me," Kane says. "You just go right ahead."

"You see, Michael, the mathematical possibility of our one day meeting, that's a relatively high number. But of our meeting as we in fact did last night and again on this flight, I'd say that number approaches zero."

"Yeah, all right," Michael says.   "I got that.   So come on, out with it--what makes you such an expert on my father?"

She forks the bit of meat into her mouth and busies herself with chewing, Michael looking on with a kind of furious rapture, his anger and desire a single wild eye mapping every contour of her magnificent, inscrutable face.

"Oh," Denise Steiner says, raising the napkin to touch at the corners of her lips, "but I am also an expert on your mother!"

Miami Beach, 12:45 P.M.

Nathan Kane examines the drama that has unfolded before him.   The black Goliath, Friday, is holding a desperately struggling Dr. Henderson in a vicelike grip.   The hyperdermic needle lies on the rug at the far wall--its contents--he can only guess--life giving or life ending?   Can she possibly be the female "hit-man" masquerading as a doctor?

Nathan leans over from where he lies on the couch and draws the woman's black bag towards him.   Mcticulously he examines its contents while the maybe Dr. Henderson continues her kicking and verbal abuse of the rocklike Friday, who stands there unflinching and unro lenting.

"I think you owe the lady an apology, Friday. I have her picture and identification here--and she is who she is supposed to be: Dr. Parthenia Henderson."

Friday releases his grip and raises his arms in surrender.

"I am sorry, my dear girl. I just couldn't take any chances where Mr. Kane is concerned."

The statuesque brown beauty takes a moment to regain her composure, straightening and smoothing the wrinkles inflicted on her white uniform at the hands of her tormentor. Then her eyes showing her full stormy fury, she whirls and strikes Friday as hard as she can, the blow landing flush on his cheek. Splat! It was totally insignificant as far as Friday was concerned like the damage likely to be inflicted by a buzzing mosquito. His expression does not change. He does not wince nor even wink an eye. He only repeats "I said I was sorry!"

The lady's anger rages unabated as her language becomes a throw-back to a vernacular street--slang calculated to be keenly understood only between one black and another. Her final words are:

"And don't call me 'your dear girl,' you mothahfucker--I am Dr. Henderson to you!"

Eventually and gradually her turbulence diminishes and her professional training regains control of her emotions. The loud words become a heatedly whispered exchange that subsides when Friday gently takes her arm and leads Dr. Henderson out of the bedroom apparently to settle the matter out of earshot of Nathan Kane and the immobilized Goldmesser, who all this while has stood transfixed and silent throughout the episode.

"So!" exclaims Goldmesser. "Now that this misunderstanding has been settled, let's get back to business. With--or without--your permission, Mr. Kane, I will resume attempting to make contact with your son, Dr. David Kane, to make him aware of your situation."

There is no response from the old man, who resignedly has turned his face inwardly toward the back of the couch as he hears the clicking of the cascading dials of the telephone. Then he rolls over so he can view the room again. Nathan Kane stares, and the significance of what is happening stares back at him, an inflamed eye that sees only the windy divide between a father and his son. For as long as he can bear it, the old man watches Goldmesser at the tele-

telephone, recording every movement of the arms and hands, the positioning and repositioning of the short legs, the small feet shifting nervously in the deep-pile carpet. And then Nathan turns himself away again, rolling away from what is happening. He faces the backrest of the couch, so that it is only the topography of the white tufted naugahyde that plays before his vision, while behind him the mild voice of reason presses forward with its strenuous purpose, going from one operator to another, from Pasadena to Los Angeles and then back down to La Jolla, in an effort to do the right thing, to do the sensible thing, to properly inform a son as to a threatening condition to his father's life. But what is it sons want of their fathers? Is it not their death? So that the sons might be the men their fathers are?

Is it the ugly truth or no truth at all? Nathan Kane wonders as he listens to Goldmesser pleading with a secretary at the Salk Institute to do something, if not to reveal Dr. Kane's unlisted number at home because, yes, he knows this is a Saturday, then to at least promise to call him this instant and tell him to telephone his father at... and then Kane hears the alien Miami Beach telephone number that the old man still refuses to recognize as his own.

Saturday, the old man thinks, it is still Saturday, a day that began like every other pastel day he's lived since leaving the high color of New York and coming South to get Rose suntanned while she died. It is a day that began with the usual walk, the usual no, the usual tree, and then everything started to go haywire--and now they're telling him old age is competing with various faceless assassins to claim his life before he can complete his plan and they are trying to reach the one person who might care the least about whether he lives or dies.

The old man considers a Saturday in California, his son David basking in magical light. Nathan Kane works for a sharper picture, a certain Mediterranean luxury of flourishing gardens, random stone pathways shaded by the strange leaves of exotic trees, an undulating swimming pool nearby, its azure waters so richly tinted as to suggest a heavenly source, a recipe mixed by angels, and there, lounging with his lovely wife in something like a gazebo, sits Kane's son, stately and resplendent in his mastery over difficult matters of science, lofty knowledge hidden away in some sacred text, a mystery shrouded in code, a modern Talmud.

Nathan looks, and what he sees is his son and then he sees his father, the man Hirsch Kapulkin rocking back and forth in secret meditation, and then the man is David Kane again--and off to the side there is another man, a shaggy beast of a fellow checked behind some kind of rough barrier, a creature too savage to be allowed closer for fear that he might chew the paper or stamp his muddy hoof upon some holy page of knowledge.

Listen to the brute snarl in stupid rage.

The ox!

The old man closes his eyes. He has never been to California. So who knows--maybe they're all lying, maybe it's just like Newark. He opens his eyes, but he does not see the little hills of white naugahyde. He sees instead the same thing he always sees when he thinks about his son for very long, the same images in the same order, the same bits of speech flashing into view like cards held up to forgetful actors--a brilliant afternoon in mid-summer, the hard ride home from New York to Newark, in every seat of the train a father eager for his offspring, maybe a little game of catch before supper, and then there's Rose on the meager patch of grass, two hands gripping the nozzle of the garden hose and directing a killing stream of water onto a square of soil that never flowers. She sees him coming up the walk and he sees her confusion, caught trying to invent life, caught with her hands unable to let go, caught with her husband coming and no way to slip toward him in graceful, loving greeting. But she does it, anyway--all clumsiness, making a mess of her shoes, getting water all over him too, but kissing him and loving him and getting back twice the love from him because of just the way she does it, all wrong and lovely.

They go inside, beating at their wet clothes, laughing, holding on, Rose calling, "Papa's home! David darling, Papa's home!"

And then somehow they're in the cramped parlor, and Nathan is just sitting in the big chair, and somehow he knows he's waiting for something, and Rose is there too, on the hassock, and she's just called out again. "David! Sweetheart! Hurry, darling, come show Papa the picture!" And Rose is smiling and smiling and saying, "You just sit there and relax, Daddy, because we got a big surprise for you," but the waiting's been going on for a little too long now and Rose's smile, that's been going on a little too long too. "David? Do you hear me, darling? Papa's here! Come show him what you got, sweetheart!" How long do they wait like that, the both of them smiling until the boy comes into the room? No, he does not come into the room exactly, but stands there where the threshold is, still fresh from his bath, hair slicked down, his hands behind his back, surveying or maybe not bothering to look at all. "Come, darling," Rose says. "Give Papa his kiss and show him the wonderful thing we have." Kane holds out his arms. But the boy moves into the room only a step or two and reaches what's behind his back to his mother. "No, sweetheart, you show it to Papa. Hurry now--climb up onto Papa's lap and let him hug you and see what you have."

But the boy shakes his head, a tentative motion and then a decisive one. He takes another step forward and drops whatever it is into his mother's hands.

"This kind," Rose says, laughing gaily. "Ach, this gorgeous kind of ours--such a piece of shyness!" But the smile is no longer there when she puts the photograph into Kane's hand.

He looks at it--his son seated on a pony and the pony standing in the Kane front yard.

"And only fifty cents, Daddy. For fifty cents, our son on a horse! Like a prince."

"It's a bargain," Kane says, and holds out his arm. "Come, son, I want to give you a kiss and hug you and ask you a few questions about this wonderful picture."

The boy retreats a step. "No."

"No? Why no?"

"I've got somethings to do--upstairs."

"Things? Well, sir, the things can wait."

"I'm already doing them. They can't."

"What's can't? Here. Come, my darling. I want to show you how much I love you and how proud you make me on this wonderful horse. Here--come, sit-- please."

The boy shakes his head. "I won't."

"Won't?" And even now Kane can feel his head coming apart, the moment still aching in him, a wind blowing across the floor of his heart. "There's a real reason for this, my son?"

"Yes," comes the boy's answer, crisp as a cracker.

"Yes? Then tell me--what?"

"You'll muss me. You're all sweaty from the city and the train, and you'll muss me and make me dirty."

It is like a bolt of ice, even now, and even now Kane shudders from the words, his heart impaled.

"So," he hears Goldmesser saying, "are you saying you will call him? You will give me that assurance? You realize this is an emergency? Professor Kane's father?"

Professor Kane--Reb Kapulkin--and between them the ox, and with the thought there comes to the old man another afternoon, only it is later and the sun is not shining and it is not summer but winter, and it is very, very cold, and the room is not filled with dappled light but with the stench of horse droppings, and the boy stands almost as tall as his father, and you can see this plainly because the boy stands very close to his father and he wants to come closer still and be held by his father but the man seems not to want it, and so the boy stands where he is, and he says, "I'm afraid," and the father answers, "The ox is afraid? This ox that kills?"

"I killed for you, Papa," the boy says, the ax still in his hands.

"For me? For me? Are you insane? You killed for yourself, murderer! Brute! Assassin! Get away from me!"

the father screams.

Nathan Kane hears Goldmesser hang up, and he swings himself around to face the small man who stands uncertainly near the telephone table, eyeglasses tipped back onto the top of his bald head.

It is then that Friday and Dr. Henderson make their entrance and it is obvious from their eyes and their expressions that the two adversaries of a brief moment ago have established a rapport, declared a truce or possibly even more so. There are certain subtle glows, shadings of smiles, and body language that are telltale when the chemistry between two people prevails over unwitting circumstance--and this seemed to be the happy case here. The crafty old man was quick to sense the transition.

"Aha!" Nathan beams and claps his hands in glee. "I see that our two representatives of the African continent have made peace with each other! No more bad language or hitting?"

Dr. Henderson smiles a bit sheepishly and then explains:

"We both agree that we both acted hastily--but I hasten to add--with your best interests in mind--and perhaps we both over-reacted."

Friday is quick to concur.

"That's true. We both got a little carried away." And then with a sideward glance at the lady to make sure he was saying the right thing. "We have made our apologies and the incident is forgotten. But we are both still very concerned about you, Mr. Kane."

Goldmesser comes forward to take up a position alongside the two of them, his head not much higher than Friday's waist.

"Just look at the three of you," Nathan Kane says, sitting up now and knocking away the hand Dr. Henderson puts out to help the old man steady himself. "Such a solemn group. So there's a hit lady coming to get me if I don't fool her and kick off first. So what? You think death is like making love and a civilized person is supposed to lie down for it. No! I'll give you Kane's advice, and I'll give it to you in a simple sentence." The old man hunches forward, gathering up his power as he looks from one to the other. "Stay on your goddamn feet!" The old man shouts. He sits back, grinning. "But to tell you the truth, it's easier said than done!"

"Do you have any numbness in your legs?" Dr. Henderson says, eyeing him.

"Can't say," the old man responds. "But when I get to feel them enough again, I'll tell you."

The old man laughs. But Dr. Henderson exchanges glances first with Friday and then with Goldmesser trying to gain a hint as to whether Nathan Kane is playing games or is serious.

"Oh my God," Nathan Kane moans, "there goes an arm!"

Dr. Henderson wheels around, almost tripping on the thick carpet. She sees the old man clutching at his throat as if strangling on poison. She starts toward him in real alarm, but when she's almost upon him, Nathan darts out an arm and draws her to him in an amorous embrace.

"Where's that nookie you promised me?" he whispers.

"You crazy mother!" she screams.

The old man slumps back against the couch, exhausted from his fun but delighted with his performance.

"What an audience!" he sighs. "Look, Friday, how about you get everyone to clear out, yes? Enough is enough."

"I'll leave only when I'm ready," Dr. Henderson says.

"You're trespassing," Kane says.

"And you're certifiable!" the woman snaps back at him.

"So who's going to pay you, Aunt Jemima? Because I sure as hell will not!"

But the woman is ready for this too. She takes a careful step closer and smiles. "The estate, you old fraud."

Nathan Kane slaps his big hand to his mouth as if appalled.

"My dear Goldmesser, and Friday, did you hear that? Did you hear this person of color addressing the master of the house in this fashion? The house of an old gentleman who has served his nation with honor, who has advised two of its presidents in times of gravest economic crisis? That such a grand old gentleman should live to hear this, this--" Kane leans over toward Goldmesser, winks and whispers, "an old fraud she called me. Tell her, Goldmesser, that I am the real McCoy--never a fraud."

"Please, Mr. Kane," the little man says, his thumb moving to adjust his eyeglasses but finding nothing there.

"On top of your head, schmuck," Kane says, still whispering and now winking the other eye.

"Please, Mr. Kane," Goldmesser begs, "this antic routine is getting nobody anywhere. You're tiring me out and you're upsetting this nice woman and, if you don't mind my saying so, you are doing yourself no credit, believe me."

"Ah," Kane says, sitting up again and then getting all the way to his feet, "now we are getting somewhere. Credit. On credit Nathan Kane here is a regular expert. This old gentleman shall tell you about credit. In my life," Kane begins, pacing off the room in a circle, his arms folded across his chest, his head tilted back as if in ponderous thought, "in the life of Nathan Kane, credit was everything, credit was all. Now to start with, in my youth and in my innocence I dispatched from this earth a full-fledged citizen of a certain rank, for he was, as you know, Mr. Goldmesser, an officer in the service of the king of all the Russias. I accomplished this unmentionable deed while in defense of my life, splitting the bastard's skull like an egg left too long in the sun. But because I was a lad who wished credit for more than was his just and honest due, I claimed other than self-defense when I sought my father's--"

The ringing of the telephone stops the old man in his tracks. His face suddenly drained of color, he looks wildly around as if choosing between unpromising options of escape.

"I'll get it," Goldmesser says.

"No! I'll get it," shouts Friday.

"No!" Kane shouts. "It's my house. Let it ring."

"Your son--" Goldmesser says, going for the phone.

"No!"

"Maybe it's my wife," Goldmesser says, grabbing up the phone before anyone can stop him. "Kane residence!" Goldmesser yells into the receiver as the old man turns away and goes into the kitchen.

Goldmesser holds the mouthpiece very close to his lips. "Hello," he says.

It is a woman's voice, very clear, very businesslike.

"Is this Mr. Kane?" she says.

"Who's calling?" Goldmesser says.

"Am I speaking to Mr. Kane?" the woman says.

"This is Goldmesser. I'm a neighbor. Who is this, please?"

"This is Mr. Kane's daughter-in-law," the woman says. "I'm calling in reply to a call that came from my husband's office. I understand Mr. Kane is unwell, and that someone there wishes to speak with his son."

"That's right," Goldmesser says. "Is Professor Kane there?"

"Actually, no," the woman says. "He seems to be impossible to locate. I

realize this is dreadful, and I wish to
say that I am personally very sorry.
Mr. Goldmesser, do you know my father-
in-law? I mean, would you characterize
yourself as a good friend, a close asso-
ciate, or the like?"

"What's your point?" Goldmesser says.

"I should like to speak freely but I
shouldn't like to do so unless it's with
someone--"

"No, no, that's all right," Goldmesser
says. "You go right ahead, but,
please, if it's not going to be possible to
get your husband on the phone or have
him do anything about this, then I must
ask you to make it quick."

"I am doing my best," the woman
says. "I don't know why the elder Mr.
Kane would even want to make contact
with his son, Dr. Kane. They have not
had anything to do with each other for
many years in even the remotest regard.
I believe Mr. Kane knows this. I have
never met my father-in-law, but it is my
understanding that the situation between
him and his son has been fixed at this
impasse for a very long time. I myself
find this unimaginable, but there is
nothing anyone can do about it."

"All right," Goldmesser says. "Is
that the message? Is that what you
wanted to say?"

"Please," the woman says.   "There is no reason to be sharp with me.   I am simply stating the facts."

"Okay," Goldmesser says, moving back to the telephone table.   He glances at the photograph, the boy on the pony.   Is this the one with the angel's face? "Look, lady, if you don't know where he is, then you don't know.   We just thought Dr. Kane should be aware of what was going on."

"Of course," the woman says.   "But if you will give me a minute more to say something.   It's difficult."

"That's right," Goldmesser says, unable to restrain himself.   "You said a mouthful--it's all difficult."

"The reason I asked about your relationship with my father-in-law is why I'm holding you on the line," the woman says, her voice still very clear, very businesslike, "Mr. Goldmesser, I trust you will view what I am about to tell you with fit discretion.   I realize this could not be happening at a worse time, but there again we are dealing with the facts.   It happens, you see, that Dr. Kane has--"

The line goes silent.   Goldmesser waits.

"Please," he says.   "Hello?"

"Yes," he hears.   "My husband is --"

Again silence.

"Mrs. Kane--please say what you have to say."

"I will say it very directly," she says. "My husband is missing. No one seems to know where he is. Now this is not at all like Dr. Kane. He is meticulous in his appointments and his punctuality. But he has not attended any of his meetings and no one has heard from him. Only foul play, an accident, or something equally dreadful would make him act this way. I don't know why I am telling you all this, a perfect stranger, but even if he wanted to just leave me, he would take the time to make arrangements for his professional commitments. He wouldn't just fly off without a word to anyone. He's never done anything like this before. It simply is out of character for Dr. David Kane!"

"I'm sorry to hear that, Mrs. Kane," Goldmesser says. "I'm sure he will show up soon. Please let him know that we would like to hear from him too!"

"I'll tell him as soon as I hear from him but please, Mr. Goldmesser, I wouldn't count on Dr. Kane making contact with his father. That would be out of character for him too."

Delta 84, 12:50 P.M.

His <u>mother</u>?

There is something starkly venomous in Denise's reference to his mother, an innuendo that snakes its way through her words until, at the end of her sentence, it rises on its coils and strikes, spitting something intended to be lethal--but what?

"My mother?" Michael says.   "But what could you possibly--?"

He does not finish--for he sees two small faces staring over the seatbacks in front.

"Do I <u>have</u> to have my peas?" the girl says.

"Two spoonfuls," Denise answers.

"What about me?" the boy says.

"The same," she says.   "Two"

"But that's not fair," the body says.

"Why isn't it fair?" Denise says, her voice given over to that metrical penetrating   musicality   that   so   captivates Michael.

"Because   I   already   <u>had</u>   some   and Cindy hasn't had any yet."

"I <u>have</u> to," the girl says.

"All right, Cindy," Denise says, "how much have you already had?"

The girl shows a finger just above the headrest.

"One pea or one spoonful?"

"Spoonful," the girl says.

"Liar!" the boy says. "She's lying, Denise she really is!"

"I have to, Denise! I swear, I really have!" the girl protests.

"Children!" Denise says firmly. "You will control yourselves. This instant!" She puts her hand on Michael's knee and smiles pleasantly at him. "Excuse me, Michael, while I restore order."

He lets the woman move past him into the aisle, helpless to resist this opportunity to appraise her again, the matchless fluency revealed to him--lower back, buttocks, thighs--a silkiness of contours that even the rough cloth of denim and cotton cannot conceal. The children disappear from view, and Michael can't make out what the woman is saying to them. But perhaps she is whispering, for appearance's sake, scolding them quietly. It would be like her, yes.

He looks at his watch, and sees that they are no more than one hour out of Fort Lauderdale, and the recognition of what this means sets something ticking in Michael's groin. He wonders how precisely it will unfold, how far from the airport Denise's hotel will be, and will they use the same taxi, and how she intends to explain his presence to the children, and will it be as exciting as the night before--or has something changed, and what she will do with the children while he and she...The ticking grows more intense with the thought. How long will he have to wait? And where? At the hotel? Is he to register there? Take a room that the two of them can use? Will there be a babysitter available to watch after the children? What? Children, he thinks, and he does not want to think it. His mind recites the names, children flung aside while their parents and comparative strangers... Cindy and Barry... and the unnamed children that Michael never had because Elaine never wanted any.

Michael shakes the vision off. He wants to see something else instead--her--and himself--the two of them--together. How much time will they have--and where? Yes, in a room he'll take somewhere in her hotel. He'll go directly there--and wait for her--wait until she has someone for the children, until they're settled for the rest of the day--and night. But when? How long will he have to wait in that room--thinking about Nat and Elaine and nearly out of his mind with waiting? Will he telephone her room? To find out what's keeping her? No, better not to--better to show at least a little restraint, a modicum of control, some last bit of

reason and balance. Better not to put
all the cards into her hands. But who
is he kidding? She already has them--
cards and spades both. And she knows
it. So all right--what's he got to lose at
this stage, anyway? He'll call. Of
course. She doesn't have the children
organized yet. But in a little while--in
a little while--a cigarette--before he's
finished smoking it, she'll come! A
knock. The door. Where will he be? At
the window looking down toward the
beach, or on the bed, staring at the
ceiling? Waiting. Going crazy--waiting.
But she knocks. Softly. Just twice.
He goes to the door--jacket off, shoes
off-shirt unbuttoned--and she, standing
there, a finger to her lips--slippers,
bathrobe. He closes the door behind
her, turns. She's mere paces away, in
here, his room, the door closed, locked,
the two of them, just standing, just
standing--no talk, nothing, enough talk,
all that talk on the plane, enough, no
more teasing, everything simple now, no
evasions, nothing ambiguous anymore, all
that playacting, all that shifting and
dodging, it's been all heading for this,
better than the sampling of the night
before, this is what it was all about,
simple, direct, their bodies, just these
bodies, and her eyes, the hair ablaze

against the white terrycloth, and her
slender feet on the carpet now, the
slippers stepped out of somewhere behind her, the feet, her feet--moving--
her foot, the bones, another, her hands
out to him, the slim fingers working at
his shirt, his trousers, her hand to his,
touching and then not touching it anymore because it is at the belt of the
robe and now there is no robe, just the
shimmering olive flesh, the belly, the
breasts, his hands at her waist, her
skin, her skin, the hips, reaching under
to cup the tensing buttocks, cool, so
cool, and raising her, up, up, and to
him, and, oh, against him, and--up--and
onto him--Denise, Denise, Denise...

"Miss me?"

It is her voice.

"They're fine now," she says.
"They're really very good children.
Terribly well behaved."

"Yeah," Michael says, his throat dry,
swallowing. "They are."

"Something wrong?" she says.

"No," he says. "Nothing. I was just
thinking."

"Yes?" Denise says. "Anything
important?"

"No."

"Oh? What about, then?" Denise
says, starting into her lunch again.

"How come they don't call you mother. They call you Denise. They call you by your name."

"Oh," she says, bringing her fork down on the little square of iced cake that serves as her dessert, "so you noticed that. My, my, how clever you are, darling. And how full of suspicion."

Miami Beach, 1:00 P.M.
Nathan Kane comes out of the kitchen grinning, a Camel gripped between his teeth, his arms flung wide, as if to scoop up Goldmesser and shovel him aside. But there is a check in the old man's right hand and he slaps it into Goldmesser's palm and then throws his arm around the little man's shoulders.

"Thank you very much!" He shouts. "Now out! And you!" Nathan Kane calls, swinging around toward the kitchen door with Goldmesser still squeezed to his side. "Doctor Nightingale! Scram! Beat it! Out of my house! Believe me, the old gentleman is grateful! Now get the hell out!--Friday! Get these people out of here!"

Dr. Henderson stands unmoving in the kitchen doorway, her hands jammed into the pockets of her crisp white uniform. Friday makes no effort to comply.

Goldmesser tries to free himself from Nathan Kane's fierce grasp, but the old man holds on hard and starts toward the front door with Goldmesser in tow.

Goldmesser, squirming hard, finally is able to catch his breath and speak.

"Let go all ready, Mr. Kane," he says. "I have to tell you about your son David."

The old man releases his grip on Goldmesser like he was a hot potato.

"My son David? What do you know of him?" Nathan Kane shouts.

Goldmesser takes a deep breath, then lets it all pour out.

"His wife called back. She says he is missing!"

"Missing? What kind of missing?"

"They can't find him anywhere to give him a message. He's disappeared-- without a note or a trace or nothing. I"m sorry to have to tell you this but I thought you should know."

Nathan Kane has a hint of a knowing sly smile on his face. He gently pats the top of Goldmesser's bald head affectionately like one would pat a dog.

"That's all right, Goldmesser. That's all right. That might be just what the doctor ordered," the old man says.

Goldmesser is obviously perplexed by

Nathan Kane's reaction and shakes his head to show his lack of understanding. Meanwhile Nathan Kane settles down heavily into an easy chair, for the moment oblivious to everyone else in the room. He thinks of David and tears appear that mar his sight. His vision clears and his eyes fall upon David's photograph and his brain stares, unbelieving. How does it happen? Nathan Kane thinks, a boy with the face of an angel, a mother, a father who loved him so much?

But Nathan Kane knows the answer. For forty, almost fifty years he has asked himself the very same question, and for almost as many years he has known the answer. It is a hard answer, one the mind instantly rejects, but which the heart as instantly affirms. It is an answer the mind can make no sense of, but which the heart, knowing better, comprehends. It is an answer that he has never uttered aloud, not even in the course of those long, terrible nights, nights when he and Rose would lie on their backs gazing up into the darkness, the question tearing at them like sharp-beaked birds, their hideous wings beating in the frozen silence of the bedroom. Except there was that one time, that time when Michael reached out at him and kept on reaching, the child's eyes desperate to see the bottom of the depth that squats malignantly between father and son.

The old man remembers what he said and how puzzled the boy looked when he said it.

You got me, maybe you got too much.

It is something the heart knows, from father to son and from father to son, but how does the mind frame it in speech? And if it could? If one could say it? What then? Would it be any different? Would anything change?

Nathan Kane turns in his chair, and he sees them all standing there, as if an audience has been summoned to sit in stern contemplation of his thoughts. Or is it his dying that they have come to watch? It is as if the three of them have been arranged in some sort of funeral formation--Goldmesser, Friday, Henderson--grim-faced mourners, grimmer-faced judges, propped stiff and vertical on the plane of wide, white carpet.

Nathan Kane again remembers the time, a time very long ago, a time that seemed like this time, the sun flooding in through the cracks in the boards, a late spring day, the time he took the ax and chopped apart a skull, believing that when he did so he would also chop away the wall that kept him from his father.

It bathed the young Nathan with a feeling he would never forget, a feeling of despair that would come again and again and keep coming, recalling the day he killed for his father and his father drove him away, and Nochem was suddenly a boy wandering west from village to village and from town to town, the towns becoming cities and the cities becoming countries, a journey that kept taking him west, until an ocean stopped him, but a ship carried him across it, all the way west to a city called New York and a country called the U.S.A. It was a feeling that would wash over Nathan Kane again, time and time again, when he would hold out his huge arms to a child of his own and the child would not come--and then the child would grow to be a man, his voice carrying all the way across a continent, to say: <u>Sorry. No thank you. Don't muss me. No touching. No dirt.</u>

The old man stands up from the chair, and the effort is like lifting a load of bricks. A whiff of dizziness blows through him, as if puffs of cloroform have been released from his joints. He grins at the sober faces etched into place before him--the brown woman scowling, the giant black man frowning, and the squat fellow with the drifting eyeglasses looking as if he is witnessing the malicious destruction of the Parthenon.

"So who called this meeting to order?" Kane shouts.

"Please, Mr. Kane," Friday says, "go back to bed."

"I will not!" he shouts.

"Just listen to him," Dr. Henderson says. "Everything at the top of his lungs."

"Now, now," Goldmesser pleads, stepping to the center of the room and running out of words as soon as he gets there.

"Now listen, Mr. Kane," Friday says, his voice achieving an unusual official directive tone. "We know you want to be up and about when Michael gets here. So why don't you just behave yourself and take it easy til then? You wanna be here when he arrives--or do you want to greet him from a hospital bed?"

"Hold on a shake!" the old man shouts. "Hospital? Bed? I don't want to hear those words. Now all of you, skip it and skip your ass right out of here!" the old man shouts. "And just for the record, and for the last time,

I'm going to tell you simply and plainly why the answer is no!"

The three of them study him with interest as Nathan Kane lets a pause elapse.

"Because I goddamn the hell <u>say</u> it is!" he shouts. He surveys them narrowly, going slowly from one startled face to the other. "Okay," the old man says, "now who's going to be the first one out of here?"

The three of them stand their ground, statues.

"All right!" Nathan Kane shouts. "Then I guess it's me that wins the prize!"

And with that the old man goes into the bedroom, puts his tennis shoes back on, returns to the livingroom, crosses to get to the coffee table, takes up the bottle of liquor, winks at the two bronze boys, and moves powerfully to the front door.

He turns to confront them once more.

"Don't forget to feed the cat!" he shouts.

Friday fairly screams at him. "You can't go out there alone! There's a killer roaming around looking for you. I'm going with you!"

The old man stands up to Friday, facing him eyeball to eyeball.

"You do--and you're fired!   You wait here!"

He flings open the door, snaps the bottle under his arm, and is gone.

Delta 84, 1:00 P.M.

"Excuse me, miss," Denise says, calling to a passing flight attendant and leaning across Michael so that the springy tissue of a breast is laid against his arm.   "Would you remove this and bring me some more coffee."

The stewardess reaches in to take her tray.

"Coffee for you too, sir?"

"What?"

"Coffee?"

"No. No thanks," Michael says.   "You know what time we'll be landing?"

"About forty minutes," the stewardess says.   "Can I get you something?"

"I'm fine," he says.   "Thanks."

When Michael turns, he sees that Denise has let down the back of her seat as far as it will go and that she has shucked off her red sandals, drawn her legs up, and lies half-reclined facing away from him, presenting him with an irresistible view of her perfect buttocks molded to her summery shorts and of the exalted poetics of line and form peculiar to the lower extremities of a well-shaped female who reposes on her side with her knees tucked up toward her chest. Michael sees everything, the soft bottoms of the slender feet, the long slim toes-- and he aches to sweep it all up and swallow it whole.

"I upset you?" he says.

There is no answer.

"I think my father called his parents by name. I don't suppose there's anything so remarkable about it. And I've always called my grandfather Nat. I'm sorry. Denise, I'm just jumpy, is the point. Skip it, okay?"

When there is no response to this, Michael takes up the brass lighter and the cigarettes. But the roof of his mouth feels raw, and he changes his mind.

He tries to sit there, just sit there and wait her out. But he can't.

"My mother? It made me feel strange when you said you knew her. You understand?"

Michael bends closer.

"Are you asleep, Denise?"

He sits back and lights a cigarette. He holds the cigarette in front of him and watches the smoke make patterns in the air. Did his mother smoke?

He can't remember.

It's a strange thing to remember at

this moment, but he recalls that she couldn't come to his bar-mitzvah. She was in the hospital. At the time the word hysterectomy conjured up all sorts of horrible connotations. But she wasn't there and he didn't understand. Would she have come if she could?

Michael was thirteen--and in the synagogue chanting words he did not understand, and everyone who came to hear him do it and to shake his hand and to assure him that now he was a man added something or other about his mother--"A wonderful woman,--to bad she couldn't come. Michael, you're a credit to your father and your good mother," "Mazel tov, Michael--and Mrs. Lefcourt and I want you to know it's a tragedy your mother couldn't come to see you bar-mitzvahed, and now that you are a man, you must be accepting of these things and try to understand."

But what was there for Michael Kane to understand?

Was illness a mystery to be figured out?

She would have been here if she could? Or would she? She wasn't Jewish and had not been enthusiastic about the whole idea. Or at least that's what Nat said.

Michael remembers the smoke and the

hotel and the noise and the dancing at the party that night. He remembers the absence of his mother. But where was his father to say that to? He remembers looking and not finding and still look-ing--because he had to talk, because something was pushing up in him and he had to get it out.

But there was Granpa at one of the long tables, and it was always as simple as that--because there was always Gran-pa whenever Michael needed someone.

"Boychik!" the old man howled. "Come sit with Mrs. Abrams and me!" And then the old man looking up at Michael and winking. "Oh, but how dreadfully forgetful of me. I meant, dear boy, Mrs. Abrams-Smythe and me."

"So you're the bar-mitzvah boy," the half-drunk woman spilled against his grandfather's chest said, trying valiantly to lift her vision to Michael's face. "Oh, and good God, look at the size of him, Nathan. Only thirteen and another giant of a Kane."

"Kapulkin!" the old man corrected. "It's the Kapulkins that are the giants around here. The Kanes I wouldn't tes-tify to."

"Oh you," the woman said, almost collapsing into Nathan Kane's lap. "You're such a wag, Nathan Kane. No wonder all the women in Washington--"

"For shame!" the old man shouted. "You silly bitch!" His grandfather winking at him again. "So, young shtarker, pull up a chair and tell us what it's like to be such a superman and only thirteen!"

"I've got to talk with you somewhere, Nat." Touching his grandfather's shoulder, the rich fabric of his winter dinner clothes.

"So talk, kiddo! Didn't we just invite you? Is there anyone in the world who would dare have a secret from this wonderful Mrs. Abrams-Smythe here?" The old man lifting the woman back into her seat and using a finger to take her under the chin and rotate her face toward him. "Pardon me, dearest person, but is it Mr. Smythe that's the Smythe or is Mr. Smythe the Abrams?" Nathan Kane looking very concerned to have an answer, the ruined woman closing one eye to hold his face in focus.

"Say that part again." Her head drifting toward the tablecloth.

"Hey, Nat, come on. I've really got to talk."

"Such disrespect. He calls the grandfather a name. You hear that, Mrs. Abrams-Smythe?"

"Nat, please."

"You hear that, lovely woman? He's got to talk, this terrific kiddo of mine." Looking up at Michael, the old man's face ruddy with drink and good spirits and his natural high color. "Sure, you've got to talk!" The powerful voice startling some people further down the table. "You've got to talk, I've got to talk. The whole shooting-match can't wait to stick a little talk in your ear!" The old man roaring, hugging the woman, peeking down her dress, hugging her hand again so that the bodice of the sequined strapless gown vees out even more and he can get a better look.

"Nat! Now! Okay?"

"Look who orders his grandfather around! Thirteen and he's already giving orders."

But then Nathan Kane is standing, the great bulk of him coming aloft, the wild white hair blazing as it rises into the light, the heavy arm raised and crooked as if to give escort, the big voice booming.

"Come, boychik, let's you and me take a little stroll to the crapper and talk things over man to man."

How long do they sit on that couch in the corridor outside the men's room talking? An hour? Two? Because he remembers the music and dancing were all over by the time they got back to the ballroom. But it wasn't the first of their great talks, talks that left Michael Kane dizzy with exhiliration, his arms and legs singing.

He remembers details--the deep burgundy velvet of the couch, the plush red carpeting that ran the length of the oak-paneled corridor, the old man looking especially regal and enormous in formal attire, their two powerful bodies side by side, the freshly lit cigarette stuck between the big man's massive fingers, the smoke dancing up, winding, coiling, flinging itself out into patterns, the old man's happiness and pride like a shower of heat that comes off him and spreads like a charmed mantle over a boy who could use it, a boy who could use the sanctuary, but whose father was never there to give it.

"So, young stuff," Nathan Kane says, "which is it? Sitting or talking?"

"Don't horse around with me, Nat. This is serious."

"Serious is it? Serious? A thousand pardons. You better excuse me while an old man arranges his brain for serious. All of a sudden it's seriousness, eh? I didn't realize. Look at it--it's thirteen, and all of a sudden, it's got to have serious. So maybe it wants a cigar because God forbid it should have to talk serious without a proper stogie in its puss." The old man winking and pulling at his crotch. "No cigar? Then maybe you'll give me your serious opinion of Mrs. Abrams-Smythe in there. You think your granpa should ditch your granma and run away with that jungeh tsatskehle? So what is your serious opinion, bar-mitzvah boy? Do me a favor and make me a gift of your wisdom in these serious matters."

Nathan Kane pulling at his crotch again and laughing.

"Come on, Nat, cut the shit. Please?"

"Listen to it. It talks dirty already. I'm sitting here like a lump on a bump waiting for this serious talk it's got to have, and meanwhile it shows off it knows a dirty word. Listen, boychik, in this life, a fella has got to amuse himself because when it comes to laughs, who can you depend on? Certainly not on the solemn youth of the nation."

The old man digging his elbow into Michael's ribs.

"Enough clowning around. I'm listening. So talk."

Not sure where to begin, not sure what he had in mind when he went in search of the old man, but striking out in the likeliest direction.

"How come you never clown around with Father?"

"Your papa? Well, kiddo, your papa is not exactly the clowning-around type."

"He's your son. How come he's not the way you are?"

The old man resituating himself in his seat, paying attention now, not ready for this, but willing to deal with it.

"Who knows from fathers and sons? People, the ordinary person, it's a mystery. Not even Einstein could figure it out. And Professor Freud, he was only guessing, but he maybe had a pretty good idea. Ah, God, when it comes to people, kiddo, go know--and when it comes to fathers and sons, don't even bother to ask. It's true--your papa and I, we've never been close. I tried, he tried, but it never worked out."

"He doesn't try. He never tries."

The old man puffing thoughtfully at his cigarette.

"No, that's not right, I don't think. Your papa's like everybody else--he's trying the best he can. So for me and for you, it's not enough, because me and you, we need something more. But him, no, he doesn't. You see? So who's to say who's right. Maybe those

that don't need so much are better off.
I look at your father and who do I see?
You know who I see, kidstuff? I see my
father--the same--a man who when it
came to people, he got along with
enough to stick in your eyeball. It's
nature. So go know. And sometimes I
think it doesn't pay to take such a long
look. You turn over a rock, you know
what you'll see? Better not to look.
Better, I think, to live and leave the
looking to the sightseers. And, besides, darling, right now your father is
a little upset--your mother... You
understand? It's a bad time for you and
a bad time for him too. So do me a
favor, and don't be so tough on him.
In this way, believe me, your papa's
doing the best he can."

The tears coming now, the feeling
working its way into his eyes, not going
back as hard as he tries to make it go
back.

"He never hugs me or kisses me or
anything like that."

The old man grabbing him very
abruptly, squeezing, mauling, suffocat-
ing him inside a wonderful embrace.

"So who needs hugs when he's got
this when he wants it, huh?"

And releasing him and slapping his
thigh and hoisting him up off the couch

and throwing his great arm over Michael's shoulder and then bending to be-
stow a kiss.

"Come, boychik--we'll go back in
there like a couple of oxen, eh? A
couple of brutes that know the way of
the world and don't give a shit because
what they got is they got each other."

He leads Michael back along the red
carpeting toward the arched entryway
into the ballroom.

"A secret, sweetheart. Your papa
and my papa, two smart men. Your
father isn't a genius? A regular scientist? But when you want to really know
something, always ask an ox. You know
why? Because all the good answers are
simple. But would a smart fella dare
give you a simple answer? Not on your
life!"

Hugging the boy against him as they
turn in through the archway.

"I love you, kiddo. If you got me,
you got enough."

Not letting go yet, and then saying
something strange and saying it fast.

"Watch out, Michael--you got me,
maybe you got too much."

It was a queer thing for the old man
to say, and it almost seemed as if there
was some threat in it. But Nathan Kane
never explained, and Michael Kane never

had the courage to ask. It frightened him then, that hurried remark, as the two of them returned to the simmering remains of the festive evening, and in a way it frightens Michael even now as he rolls the statement around in his mind looking for a way into it and thus into a secret the old man knows.

You got me, maybe you got too much.

It makes Michael Kane think of Denise and he is about to lean over her again and try to pry her out of her silence when the seat-belt sign lights up and the captain's voice sounds over the public-address system, the announcement wedged into that run-on, lazy, indifferent drawl Michael suspects pilots are carefully taught right along with how to operate the big commercial jets.

"Ladies and gentlemen, this is your pilot, Captain Ross, speaking. We'll be making our descent and approach soon, and it looks like we're going to be experiencing a little choppy air on the way down, so I've turned on the seat-belt sign. Please return to your seats and observe the sign. We're on time and should be at the gate at about one-twenty-three, Day-light Savings Time. It's clear in Fort Lauderdale and they're reporting ninety-nine degrees at the airport. It's been a pleasure to serve you, and the crew and I thank you for flying Delta."

"Your seat belt," Michael says to Denise, bending close to her.

Her voice is oddly faraway, softer, somewhat girlish.

"You do it," she says.

"With pleasure," Michael says, and turns in his seat to strap her in.

"First the children," she says.

"Yeah, sure," he says, and gets up and goes to the seats in front. He hunkers down in the aisle. "Okay, gang, time to get your seat belts fastened again." The girl obeys promptly, but the boy seems baffled by the apparatus, and Michael reaches in to work the buckle for him, loving the chance to do this, to do something for a child, for any child.

"How's that?" Michael says, reaching over to the window seat to test the boy's belt. "Everybody all snug?"

The children nod. "You're not the pilot, are you?" the girl asks.

Michael is thankful for the moment that Cindy does not seem to recognize him from the awful thing that happened the night before. Maybe it's because he has his clothes on--or maybe it's because she does not want to remember. A nagging thought flashes through his mind: How many men has Cindy seen in his mother's bed? Then he thinks: what difference does it make. She's not a virgin and neither are you.

"No, no," Michael says. "I'm a passenger, just like you guys. I'm the fella sitting right in back of you with your mommy, who's sort of sleeping and said I should do this. Okay?"

Michael helps them adjust their headsets again, and then he ruffles the little boy's hair and goes back to his seat.

"Your turn," he says to Denise, hovering over her.

She raises her head and turns it a little, so that her lips are close to his ear.

"Touch me," she says. "Don't let them see. But touch me."

What she says sends a crackling tremor coursing through him, a long jagged wave of feeling that crests and crashes in his legs.

"Here?"

"Here, " she whispers.

He reaches around her with both arms and lowers his chest over her, his hands feeling for the ends of the seat belt, catching hold of the buckle on one side and then letting it go to move to the belly just above it, and then his whole hand unfolding against her belly and pressing down and skidding to a resting place below the zippered fly.

"Inside," she whispers and he can feel her hand brushing past his to reach up and undo the single button at her waist.

Michael can't see, but he can feel the fabric give, and just barely hears the zipper buzz open.

He puts his lips against her ear.

"This is crazy, Denise."

She does not answer, but moves her body slightly so that she is facing completely away from the aisle, and then Michael feels her cool fingers tugging at his wrist and guiding his hand up to where the zipper has come wide enough apart.

It is her skin, just that--and it is-- unbearably taut, a contradiction to be found in only very special women.

"Touch me," she murmurs, turning her face toward the backrest, and Michael lets his fingers creep down until they reach a delta of curly hair. He pauses there for a moment relishing the soft mound. Then as he prepares to move further her head comes abruptly up and she turn to face him.

"Did you buckle the children in?"

He does not speak. He cannot speak. He moves his chin against her cheek to say yes.

"Aren't they good children?" she whispers.

Again he moves his chin against her, his fingers arrested where they lie in readiness.

She moves her head again, bringing her lips against his chin.

"You and the children, you have a lot in common," she says.

Has he heard her right? But he gestures with his chin again, as if to acknowledge, as if to confirm his understanding of this.

"Yes," the woman whispers against his face, "you are so trusting and your needs are so basic. You have full confidence in your instincts about me--yet you really know nothing about me."

His right hand rests on the smooth stone lying just above the divide between her legs, its subtle convexity fitted to the hollow of his palm. His left hand spreads against the small of her back, the fingers opened wide over the contoured flesh.

"What you say is true," Michael says. "But I can wait til you are ready to tell me--as long as I know this is what I will be waiting for."

Her lips lift away and then touch again at a spot between his ear and chin. She nips a bit of skin between her teeth and he feels it pulled up and down as she nods her head in answer.

"I'm worth waiting for--and it won't be much longer."

She moves her lips to his earlobe, wets it, and, sucking, draws it slowly into her mouth.

He feels suction, the woman's tongue slipping back and forth across the underside of his earlobe, and then he feels something else, something Michael is not the only one to feel, something felt by everyone aboard Delta 84, and behind him, in response to it, someone cries out in fear as the aircraft is slammed from below, shudders violently, and is slammed again. In one motion Michael pushes himself away from Denise and wrenches around to look back down the aisle. He sees a stewardess two rows back, one hand gripping a seatback to steady herself, the other hand holding an empty tray. At her feet, a styrofoam cup rolls part way across the aisle and then starts heading toward Michael as the aircraft pitches crazily forward and noses down.

The stewardess sees him looking; she smiles sheepishly, mouths the words "Sorry," and shrugs--and then her expression changes to something with more alarm than apology in it as the aircraft

yaws to the side and then jerks through
a fast cadence of small hard bumps, the
effect one feels in an automobile whose
brakes are being lightly pumped for fear
that two sudden a deceleration will send
everything careening out of control.
Michael looks at the stewardess's face
and then at the faces arrayed behind
her, all of them impassive, solemn,
featureless, not unlike the faces of
first-graders on the opening day of
school or those of men grouped around a
poker table where the stakes are too
high and a new hand's being dealt. It
is when he realizes that he's looking up,
that the view toward the tail carries
one's vision up an incline that steeply
rises, it is only then that Michael returns his attention to the stewardess and
thinks to call out to her, to ask her
what's going on. But he doesn't. It
seems to him that asking something might
also be tempting something, and he
moves to face forward like the rest.

"What is it?" Denise says.

"Beats me," Michael says, reaching
for the cigarettes and lighter. He offers
her a cigarette. She takes it and then
takes the light he offers her. "Maybe
you better get your seatback up and get
yourself strapped in," he says.

But she doesn't answer. She's on

her feet and pushing past him into the
aisle, almost falling as the airplane
sways wide to the side again, a kind of
woozy swimming notion, as if bolted
plates of steel have transformed themselves into something organic, a gel-
atinous substance that shimmies lazily
through dense liquids.

Michael sees Denise step around to
the seats in front and then bend out of
view. He looks out the window, an
oblong of sickening grey as the plane
descends through depths of cloud, a fine
mist blowing across the glass. He leans
farther over, to check back toward the
wing, but his seat is too far forward to
see anything but more grey. When he
turns back to use his ashtray, he sees
the same stewardess leaning in behind
Denise, smiling and gesturing, and then
Denise is visible again, and although
Michael can't hear, it's clear she's being
told to return to her seat. She bends
back to the children again and then she
quickly reappears, falling against the
stewardess, the two women then thrown
all the way across the aisle as the aircraft suddenly lifts and lifts, quite as if
cables are yanking it straight up, re-
moving aircraft and passengers and crew
from the world of motion and time.
Michael flips open the seat belt and goes

forward on one knee into the aisle, standing and bringing both women up with him.

"I'm fine," the stewardess says, embarrassed, pushing at Michael's shoulder. "Now, if you will both just get back in your seats and buckle in, I'll get to my station and everything will be O.K."

"What's happening?" Michael says, keeping his voice low.

"It's nothing," the stewardess says, still pushing at him. "Everything's quite under control. We're making our descent into Lauderdale and there's just a little weather going down."

"You call this a little weather?" He says, letting Denise go around him toward her seat.

The stewardess gives Michael a sharp look and then moves on down the aisle. He starts to swing into his own seat, but stops himself to step back where he can see the two children.

"Hey, you two!" he calls down to them. "Everything ship-shape up here?"

The girl nods, and when the boy sees his sister nod, he nods too.

"Yeah," Michael says, grinning, "the thing of it is, part of the fun going to Miami is to have a little roller-coaster ride just in case you're not going to be able to get to go to Disney World.   You customers going to get to go to Disney World?"

The girl shakes her head, and then the boy follows suit.   "We've been to Disneyland," the girl says.

"No kidding," Kane says, leaning down.   "All the way out in California?"

"It's not in California," the boy says. "It's in Anaheim."

The girl makes a sour face at her brother and then flashes a knowing look to Michael.   "Anaheim's in California," she says.   "He knows that.   He's just being silly."

"Yeah, well," Michael says, straightening up now, "every once in a while a fella's got a right to be a little silly if he wants to.   Right, champ?"

The boy nods.

"You bet," Michael says, looking back at their mother, who sits leaning forward, listening.   "Guess I'll get back to my seat now and enjoy my end of the ride.   Don't want to hog all your fun up here."

He can't help himself.   Once again he puts his hand to the crown of the little boy's head and lightly washes it through the long, silky hair.   He turns back to his own seat, and buckles himself back in next to Denise.   "This ride is very scary--like life itself. It reminds me of the tightrope we all walk everyday-- holding on--while almost falling off."

Her voice is very changed, not so penetrating, not so musical. Michael is surprised by the sudden revelation of a philosophical dimension to her person- ality. Then Michael hears her gasp a little as the aircraft gives way to a brusque drop, and abrupt absence of everything save the sense of sudden and sustained floorlessness. But it lasts no more than three seconds, each a lifetime long.

Denise laughs a dry laugh, her face not smiling.

"You put things on, you take things off--shoes, clothes, passions, hatreds, lovers, one guise after another, until all of them are worn out--and then you take off your life or someone robs you of it and death is thrust upon you. Isn't that what happens day after day, until all the days are over?--Isn't that what's happening to your grandfather--and to all of us?"

Michael says nothing in reply. It's too much to manage all this at once, the aircraft's alarming progress through the sky, the crazy thing Denise said just before the chaos hit, and now this, yet another abrupt change in her manner, as

if other insights to her personality still
wait to be revealed.   Michael listens to
her and he studies her face as she
talks.   The frightening episode has had
a decidedly sobering affect on her, very
different from what he's heard and seen
thus far. He searches for a way to perceive her anew, to convince himself that
what she is showing him now is not still
another pose but finally something very
real.

Miami Beach, 1:30 P.M.
Nathan Kane is into the elevator and on
the way down before they can try to
stop him.   He steps into the lobby and
cuts   through   the   press   of   residents
going to and from lunch in the restau-
rant located on the ground floor of the
building. He heads for the entryway at
front, his stride muscular again, his
carriage erect, almost martial, the fifth
of clear liquor propped under his arm,
the neck of the bottle grasped with his
opposite hand, so that the effect is
rather like that of a military officer
reviewing the troops, his swagger stick
held smartly at parade position.   The
other residents see him coming and they
move to get out of his way, for many of
them have had the fright of the man's
thundering No! and those that haven't

have heard the reports of the crazy old
bastard, that horse of a gangster, whose
violence is brought down from the penthouse onto the tranquil streets of Bal
Harbour every morning at eight on the
dot.

The old man stops at the little office
maintained by the crew of doormen, and
he collars the man in charge.

"You'll do me a favor, Joe," Nathan
Kane says, his face flushed with excitement, his white hair flying. "I got a
kid, about thirty--you can't miss him.
An ox like yours truly, only his hair
ain't so white already. Are you listening?"

The man nods, his head craned
uncomfortably back to see Kane's face
because the old man holds Joe close to
him to whisper.

"Yeah, yeah, I'm with you," the man
says, "but I don't get it. This morning
I saw them cart you in here like a
corpse and for a couple of hours we had
an ambulance down here at the ready.
So what's the story, Mr. Kane? You got
some magic pill?"

Nathan Kane turns away from the
lobby, lowers his hand to his crotch,
grabs, lets go, and winks. He leans
down conspiratorially. "Hey, come on,
Joe, you know how it is. I was all set

to croak and then I figured how about I tear off just one more piece of ass first." He nudges the doorman in the ribs, waits for his laugh, gets it, and goes on.

"Now look, Joe, the kid's name is Michael, Michael Kane, and as I said, you can't miss him, so you tell your boys who to look out for, and anyway, he'll be asking for me, right? So when he shows, which will maybe be anytime, you tell him I'm out on the beach, out on the end of that rock jetty, and to come on the hell out there and collect me. You got it?"

The man knows Kane, knows all about the stories that are told about the old man. But a person of his years going out on that rock jetty? All the way out? And isn't that a bottle of whiskey he sees under Kane's arm?

"Yeah, sure," the man says, "but do you think that's such a hot idea, Mr. Kane? I mean fooling around on those rocks? Young guys, locals, real fisherman characters, they get themselves pretty busted up out there I hear, and twice since I've worked this job, which is only three years, guys've drowned."

Again Nathan Kane winks and grins. "No shit. Well, fact of it is, the nookie I've got waiting for me only likes to do

it on the rocks. So you just do as I
say, hear? Michael Kane--you send him
out there to get me. And now listen--
anybody else asks you or your boys
where I am, you're deaf and dumb, yes?
We have a deal?" Kane says, slipping a
five-dollar bill into the head doorman's
hand and waiting for the man's assurance.

"Yeah, I guess," the doorman says,
pocketing the money.

"Good," Nathan Kane says, turns
around, goes back across the lobby,
exits through a side door toward the
pool, and jogs past the few residents
that are daring the heat of the day, sitting safely out of the sun's angry eye
under umbrellas set up over card tables.
He gains the concrete stairs that lead
down to the beach, and, slowing to a
walk now, the old man starts slogging
through blazing sand so fired by the
August heavens that it scorches right
through the rubber soles and canvas
uppers of his shoes. The close, wetted,
roasting air crawls over him like a thing
with life, yet Kane seems not to notice
it, or anything else that announces the
torporous weight of full midday.

The whole wide beach is deserted as
far as the old man can see in either
direction, save for, in the distance to

the north, a burly young man fishing,
casting into the heavy surf, and, near-
er, behind Nathan Kane, a young woman
has also left the Bal Harbour pool area
and makes her way to the shallows that
lie to the leeward side of the jetty.   The
old man heads in that direction, angling
from the huge pastel building behind him
toward the black line of rocks and
boulders that runs straight out from the
beach into the ocean for well over two
hundred yards, a distance as great as
that which the old man must cross from
the last stair down to the beach to
arrive at the base of the first black
boulder.   It is a hard trek through soft
sand in any circumstance, but in this
heat it is like a walk through flame.
Yet Nathan Kane feels a wild surging of
energy, the blood jumping in his veins.
His massive form leans into the walk,
and the sun beats against him, the white
of his clothing seeming to vibrate in the
glare as if it buzzes with agitated fibers
and thread.   He holds the bottle of
liquor as he held it when he marched
through the gaping traffic in the lobby,
working the neck up and down as he
plies the hot sand, very like a man
pumping his armpit to crank his body
into motion.

By the time he makes it to the jetty,

the old man has used up the energy he
thought he'd have for this thing. It
had come from nowhere, amazing him,
and now it has escaped back to where it
came from, emptying him. The first big
rock, a foul-smelling boulder that looks
angered by the heat, looms up in front
of him, too high to climb just yet. He
sags against it, and brings the bottle
down, holding it at his knee by the
neck. He breathes deeply, and a quick,
slicing chop of pain rips a tear somewhere high inside his chest. Beach flies
swarm around the boulder, and bent
over as he is, Nathan Kane sees the
chunks of dead fish and sections of
mouldering crab that have collected at
the base of the big black rock, pushed
there by the action of the surf and
stopped by the mass of granite that
plunges into the sand.

The pain subsides and his lungs fill
with fresh air. He heaves himself forward off the rock and stands straight
again, turning to face the thing he's
made up his mind to scale. He reaches
the bottle to a level place high up, and
then he lifts his foot to the start of the
natural path to the top. It takes him
minutes to make his way all the way up,
and his legs are bruised, one elbow
actually bleeding, but not very much,

The young woman in the shallows seems to be monitoring his progress. A sack of sea shells is rigged so that it hangs suspended from her neck.

Perhaps the old man does not notice her. At least he doesn't seem to. He takes up the bottle of whiskey, the sweat dripping from his nose when he leans over, and then the old man stands all the way up and turns to face in the direction straight out. He starts picking his way forward, choosing his footing with care, going gradually and steadily from rock to rock, until he is well beyond the depth even the strongest swimmers risk. He stops for a time and catches his breath, for an instant turning his head to look back at the huge pink building behind him. From where Nathan Kane stands he can see the penthouse perched on top. It is the first time he's seen the thing this way, from the outside looking in. He wonders if the three of them are still there, still frozen in formation on the white carpet. Perhaps even at this very minute his beloved Rose is boarding an elevator up to join them, a newly made jar of borcht or schav or gefulte fish in one hand, a simple flower in the other. Of course! That's exactly what's happening this very instant, Rose rising to sit and wait

for him up there, returned from where
ever she went away to for all those long
terrible months.

Tears make their way into the old
man's eyes, and he turns again to the
distance in front. The sun seems to be
sucking steam off the surface of the
water out there, and the world of endless ocean and bottomless light looks
misted and hazy, queerly turbulent and
sleepy at the same time. Nathan Kane
starts forward again, his progress slow-
er now, for now the surf hurls itself
against the jetty broadside, and
swatches of water are thrown high and
then fall, slapping the rocks hard, like
wet clothing slammed down by a raging
woman fed up with doing wash. He cautiously keeps his eyes on his shoes,
fitting his rubber soles into the safest
places to try--but even so he slips three
times and almost goes all the way off
before he's made it all the way to the
last rock, a boulder even larger than
the one he started off on.

For a while he just stands there,
looking out to the shimmering sea, and
then he lowers himself slowly, letting
himself down in cautious stages, so that
at last he is seated on the very edge of
the rock, his long legs hanging over the
side, the charging surf mere inches

below his feet.

He holds the bottle out in front of him and sees it is almost half full, and then he raises the neck to his mouth and yanks out the cork with his teeth, blowing it back out from his lips so that it floats off to the water below, bobbing against the base of the rock until the next swell of ocean moves it back beyond him and well out of sight.

"You're going the wrong way, sucker," the old man mutters, and then he hoists the bottle to his lips and up-ends it, getting five good gulps down into his gut, the clear whiskey scalding as it makes its descent, so that Nathan Kane can almost feel the lake of fire pooling on the floor of his stomach.

"Glick and Mahzel!" the old man shouts at the ocean, and then, when a lone gull swoops past his vision, catching the air and sailing off to the north Nathan Kane shouts again: "You heard me! Glick and Mahzel!" He laughs and pulls again on the whiskey, wheezing fitfully when the bottle comes away from his lips. "What's the matter, bird! You don't speak Yiddish? Ah, God," Kane murmurs to himself, shaking his head and smiling, "where are the good old Jewbirds of yesteryear?"

He tries to lean back on his elbows,

but it hurts where he scraped himself,
and, anyway, the rock is too sharp and
too hard. He turns his head all the way
to the left and slowly, turning back
again, scans the line of the horizon,
finding nothing, not even a faraway
freighter or tanker steaming north.

"Bupkis," he says. "Just me and a
rock and you, ocean. And of course
this old pal of mine, here," Nathan Kane
says, raising the bottle of liquor and
drinking again.

Surf splashes up onto his legs, wet-
ting the white cotton trousers and cooling him.

"Thanks," the old man says, nodding, and in that instant he is visited
by a flashing sequence of images that
bring tears to his eyes again.

"Oh, God," he says, remembering,
and drinking from the bottle once more,
looking out to sea as he unreels the
event in his mind--the filthy stinking
hold of the ship and all the riffraff
crowding close in fear, Kane still
Kapulkin and only seventeen years old,
but a head taller than anybody there,
and therefore the first to see the woman, big-breasted, tall, like himself,
and also, like himself, hair that looked
as if she'd been born on the surface of
the sun itself.

There were hundreds down in there, squashed together deep below-decks, Jews and whatever other drek were risking the death that came from life on board for the life you had a crack at if you lived through the crossing from Liverpool to New York. The stench was unimaginable, the human outpourings that spilled from armpits and crotches and stomaches and lungs and bowels. People sprawled everywhere, sick and dizzy with the motion of the ship, with hunger and thirst, and the awful air, but the woman, like Kane, stood, her head leaned back against an iron pole, and everything she was wearing was black, and her skin was very white, and she was gazing at Kane, and she was so very tall, deepchested and wonderfully regal and tall.

That night they fled together to the freedom of the deck, stealing up the spiraling iron stairways, the clean sea air reaching down the steps to them and drawing them higher and higher to the wide open sky and the crashing symphony of tossing water and starlight, Kane following the woman up, his eyes fixed on the swaying of her hips as she climbed just in front of him, her black skirts caught up tight against her. Out on deck they hunched and crept along to a good place well forward where they could hide themselves and pass the night just breathing and undetected.

"So?" she said, when they were lying side by side, "you have a name?"

"Nochem."

"And where are you from, Nochem?"

"Horka."

"Ah. And you go to America?"

"Yes."

And a moment or so later.

"Nochem? Is that a name for a Jewish boy?"

"I think so."

"No, no," her voice teasing. "You are not a Jewish boy."

"Yes. Of course I am."

"No, no, it is not true."

He was speechless, crazy with wanting, unable to understand her playfulness.

"No, no, you are taking advantage of a poor Jewish girl. A boy like you, so big, so strong. You are not even from Horka, I fear."

And later, when she had turned away from him, and he lay against her back with his face in her hair.

"How old are you, Nochem?"

"Twenty."

"Twenty? I don't believe it. You are fibbing again."

"I swear."

"Mustn't swear. It is a sin. Ach, a Christian boy and he sins."

Feeling her back against him, the whole length of her, the shapes that went in and out, the lazy rocking of the ship, her body moving and rocking against him.

"And you? Are you twenty also?"

"I? I am twenty-three--and therefore too old for a boy of twenty."

"No, not too old."

Her back pressing against him, fitting itself to him, the ship lifting and falling.

"No, not Jewish no."

"It is true. I am. I swear."

"He swears. For shame. But if you were a Jewish boy, you would prove it."

The two of them moving with the movement of the ship, everything quiet save for the speech of air and water all around them.

"I will quote from the Talmud. You'll see."

"No, no, no, that proves nothing. A smart Christian lad perhaps. Who knows? Ah, yes, they taught you Jewish things so that you could deceive a Jewish girl. It happens. No, no, if you were a Jewish boy, you could prove it."

His mind racing, his heart running

still faster.

"How?   There is no way to prove such a thing."

"Oh yes.   Oh, yes.   I show you."

Her hand coming back and then pressing down along the front of him and then pushing its way inside his trousers, taking him into it like a mouth swallowing him whole, testing and kneading until a great dizziness came over him and then leaped into a powerful buzzing like circles opening out from a central circle that seemed to be all over him at once, and her voice very soft now, a whisper, "Yes, yes, you are what you say," and "Yes, yes, it is really all right," and then just, "Nochem, Nochem, Nochem," as she let him go and moved herself to face him and there was suddenly nothing but things opening and the ship rocking and a feeling that he was collapsing into himself and shattering apart, going and coming, at once.

Just before dawn they kissed one last time and started back, his hand at her waist as they crept back to the first stairway down.   It was then that Kane realized he'd never asked for her name-- and when he asked, she gave it, a name like the woman she was.

Rose.

Delta 84, 1:30 P.M.

The aircraft drops free of the clouds like an exotic dancer gradually disrobing, her fingers trailing lengths of the gauzy stuff unraveling from her torso as she flings herself across the sky and pays out veil after veil behind her. The cabin is once again bathed in devastating light, Denise's hair inviting it and glowing with renewed brilliance. Michael's fingers ease where he grips the armrests, and everything seems to him freshly lustrous, scrubbed and bristling with life.

The NO SMOKING sign blinks on, and the P.A. system briefly crackles and then smooths to the practiced, even sentences of a flight attendant announcing landing instructions, her remarks concluding with an apology for the discomfort experienced by the passengers as the airplane made its descent.

"Gee, I didn't know that was Delta's fault," Michael says, striving for a cheerful effect. "Me, I thought it was Thor or Zeus, or maybe Nathan Kane welcoming us in."

"He's like that, isn't he?" Denise says, pulling her carry-all into her lap.

"Nate? That old man is thunder in shoes and socks. Yeah, he's like that, all right. You'll see."

"I hope so," Denise says, dropping the paperback into the satchel.

Michael turns to her, to see her profound beauty again, the light fully illuminating the delicate sculpturing of her face. "You hope so?"

"I just hope he's all right," the woman says.

Michael feels rushed back to the reality of earth in more ways than one. Again she infers that she may know more than is possible.

He hears the rush of air as the pilot begins lowering the flaps, and then he hears Denise again, her voice raised slightly to speak over the noise.

"You, dear Michael, are obviously rushing to his side. It logically follows that either your grandfather is not well or he is in some sort of danger--and you are a white knight to the rescue."

He hears the landing gear release and lock into position, and then he hears himself say: "You have a wonderfully deductive mind for such a beautiful lady. You should have been a lawyer or private detective or CIA agent--instead of whatever you are."

Denise smiles coyly. "Maybe I am."

"Maybe you are what?" Michael persists.

"Maybe I am all those things. We will

just have to wait and see, won't we?"

"Yeah," Michael says, thinking, considering, feeling the pressure against his back as the aircraft settles in for its glide to the runway and the engines kick onto landing power.

"I guess so," he continues. "I've reconciled myself to being told when you are ready to tell me."

The tires touch tarmac, grab, and then roll, as the heavy machine hurtles along the runway and the engines reverse and the aircraft slows, and then starts its long crawl to the receiving gate. It is not until they have come to a halt and passengers are standing and collecting their belongings that Michael speaks again.

"What about tonight," he says. "Are we still on for tonight?" His voice is more anxious than he would like it to be.

"It all depends," Denise says, undoing her seat belt and standing. "I have to make two phone calls. Then I will let you know."

"What about the grandfathers, mine and the kids?" Michael says, getting to his feet now and letting her move past him into the aisle. "Are we still going to see them together tomorrow like we decided earlier." Michael did not want to lose that opportunity.

"That too," Denise says, "depends on the phone calls."

Kane sits back down. For some reason, he does not want to leave this seat. He has the feeling that to do so would be to leave something vital behind, something precious, a small item that a hurrying man might overlook.

"All right," he says. "I guess it's time to go."

He watches as she gathers up the children and moves them ahead of her into the line of departing passengers. He leaves his seat, after picking up the big brass lighter and her pack of cigarettes. He slips them both into the pocket of his jacket. Then he takes off after her. Michael accompanies Denise and her children through the corridors of the crowded terminal following the signs for baggage pickup. An escalator carries them down to the ground floor and they stand and wait til finally the conveyor belt grinds and begins to produce the baggage from Delta Flight #84. The children are pressed to her legs and pointing to their various pieces of luggage as they appear. Finally they have all been collected. They present their tickets for identification to the guard, get a red cap to handle the luggage, and start toward the "EXIT" doors. Denise pulls up short when she spots an enclosed phone booth and signals that she is going to make her calls now. She enters, perches herself on the seat, motions for Michael to hold Cindy and Barry's hands, and starts to dial.

Michael cannot help but sense the warmth that the tiny fingers generate enclosed in his mammoth paws. How like a natural family unit the four of them are. He likes the feeling and sincerely hopes something will come of it.

Michael casually turns and watches Denise inside the glass cage. She has dialed many numbers--obviously a long distance call he thinks. He wonders if she is requesting instructions as her speech is quite animated and then she is quiet--listening and nodding her head intently. She finishes and flashes a glorious smile to him and the children. Then she deposits coins again. She dials. Fewer numbers this time--a local call. She listens hard for what seems like a long time but there is no conversation. The party does not seem to answer. Denise seems upset as she jams the phone back on its hook and opens the door. She is practically running before she speaks. Michael starts after her dragging the children with him.

"Let's go," she says. "I don't like it!"

Michael tries to catch up with her.

"Hold on a minute! Give me a break! What don't you like?"

Denise stops and turns to face him.

"Oh I am sorry. I didn't mean to run off and leave you with the children."

"Tell me. What don't you like?" Michael persists.

"Your grandfather, Nathan Kane. His phone is out of order. Let's go!"

"Just a moment!" Michael is astounded. "You better explain that one. My grandfather has an unlisted phone. And why would you call him anyhow?"

"No time for questions now, Michael I'll explain on the way. Let's grab a cab."

They pile into a taxi and take off.

"Where to?" the cab driver asks.

"Give him directions to Nathan Kane's place." Denise says.

"Bal Harbour apartments!" Michael says automatically, not understanding any of this.

He turns to look at the shopping malls and apartment buildings and motels racing past. He tries to settle himself by taking a deep breath.

"Well?" he begins.

"Well? she responds. Denise still seems anxious, almost eager. She seems to be urging the taxi on with the rhythmic rocking of her foot.

"You said you would tell me on the way?" Michael watches her closely. Will she finally open up or will she continue her evasive action. The answer was soon forthcoming.

"Oh, did I say that? I meant as soon as we get there. You can wait a while longer, can't you darling?"

She pats his cheek gently as if to ease the pain of his anxiety. Michael cannot help thinking for the moment how much he would love to paddle her infuriating--but lovely buttocks. But he resigns himself to a wait and see condition, since there seems to be no alternative. The woman is determined to play this out to the hilt--her way. Well, the only good thing about it, he thinks, is it can't be much longer. Everything would have to come together very soon.

He can't wait to get out of the taxi, and neither can Denise. When the car pulls up into the Harbour House driveway, Michael and she are out the door before one of the attendants can get to it to open it for them. He pays the driver, and is not yet inside the building when he's stopped and asked if his name is Kane.

"Right," Michael says, a little surprised, eager to keep moving and get
upstairs.

"I'm Joe. Your father--"

"My grandfather?"

"Yeah, your grandfather," the man
says. "Mr. Kane. He says you'll find
him on the beach out on the jetty. He
wants you to go out there and get him.
Myself, I don't think--"

"He's where?" Denise interrupts.

Joe looks at them, satisfied. "You
see my point?"

"Goddamn, the sonofabitch is something, isn't he?" Michael says, smiling.

"It's a fact," the man says. "I told
him not to go out there--and I'm telling
you. It's dangerous as hell."

"Right," Michael says, "Point me to
the way!"

The doorman looks uncertain. But he
studies the big, blond man looming in
front of him, and he sees that this Kane
is like the other one, and there is no
sense arguing. He leads quickly to the
beach area and points out to the jetty
with Michael, Denise and the children
right behind him.

"I'm going out there. Denise, please
wait in the lobby with the kids," Michael
says.

Denise shakes her beautiful head vehemently. "No way!" she says. "I'm going with you. Joe will keep an eye on the kids. O.K." She addresses the latter to the doorman, who--like most people--is overcome by her beauty and is powerless to deny her anything.

Joe nods his acceptance and Michael and Denise plunge out into the torrid sand and sun toward the jetty.

Miami Beach, 3:00 P.M.

The August sun takes Nathan Kane up in its meaty fist and squeezes, driving the sweat out of him in furious spills, down cheeks and arms, back and legs, until he sits slumped forward and swimming in his own fluids. He breathes with his jaw slung open, like a slaughterhouse beast seconds shy of succumbing to the blow of the kill-bar that an instant ago entered, and then withdrew from, his brain. The strength pours from the old man, and yet he feels himself curiously alive, as if as he shirks from the work of the sun's violence, something inside him grows correspondingly larger. He feels a weird elation, eruptions of energy coursing through him, a mad impulse to stand and leap from the top of this rock. Would he fall? Would his body curve back to earth and send him down into the waters and death? Or would he rise and rise, soaring effortlessly, sailing in great widening circles through the roof of the sky?

He sits where he is, mouth open, eyes closed, seeking himself spiraling up, the rushing air cooling him until, in the vast night of space, he vanishes, invisible but forever alive.

"I'm behaving like a fool," Kane says aloud, then he laughs, and thinks to himself, So what else is new?

He raises the bottle and swallows.

"Ah, God," he says. "Good."

He sets the bottle down carefully, and then leans back, with his hands thrust out behind him.

"Anybody listening?" Kane shouts at the ocean. "Because the ox got a couple a things to say--just for the record, mind you! As I said before I'm a fool-- and there's no fool like an old fool! Nobody is coming!--not Michael--and I really didn't expect David--but I tried-- and I failed! My plan with my book is a flop--I have to confess--and before I die I must also confess--Dr. Henderson is right--I am an old fraud. I never intended to write a whole book and squeal on my old friends no matter how dirty their hands were--listen--were mine so clean? I just gave the publisher a few juicy morsels to whet his appetite and get the publicity--and then made sure that both Michael and David were inform- ed that my life was in danger. Hey, listen, can you blame an old man whose time is running out for trying to bring his son and his grandson back together and the two of them here? But it looks like neither of them care. Nobody is coming! Not Michael--and just between the two of us, God--like I said before I really didn't expect David. But the plain truth of the matter is I couldn't just let it all end like this without trying--trying to end this crazy cycle of Kapulkins and Kane's. I thought that just maybe--when you peeled away enough of the ego and the vanity and the old bullshit and you reached the meaty core--down where they live in their heart of hearts--they would both forget the past and come running to try to save me--but I was wrong. What can I tell you? I was wrong! They are preoccupied. Michael is on the outs with his wife--so he is probably shacked up with some broad--and David is missing-- -probably hiding away in some mountain retreat to contemplate his navel or some other important scientific phenomenon. I tried and I failed--could I do less--being

who I am? So let them work it out
themselves between them--Michael and
David--after this body of mine has
grown cold. But didn't I have to
try--the only way I knew how? Maybe
the whole thing never happened--good-
bye and good luck! But for you and
me, ocean--for us it's all one long
gehakteh day, and the sun never goes
down till you're dead! So what else do
you want to know?" Nathan Kane
shouts.

He takes up the bottle and drinks
again.

"Ah, skip it!" he yells, gesturing
with his other hand. "Go talk to an
ocean." Kane brings his hand back to
his face to flick sweat from his eyes,
and he hears a voice shout "Watch it!
You trying to drown me, old man?"

Nathan Kane jerks his head around.
Is he hearing things?

"Jesus God Almighty!" he shouts.
"Well, it's the goddamn kid! You didn't
forget me?"

"Hey, Nat!" Michael Kane shouts,
hunkering down next to the old man.
"How the hell are you, big fella?"

They fling their arms around each
other and for a long time they embrace
this way, gently rocking each other back
and forth. There are tears in their

eyes, but neither man sees the tide of emotion that is sweeping through the other, and when at last they let each other go, they both remember that they are not alone. Denise--the lovely Denise--her athenic figure outlined in the ocean wind with her spray-sparkled hair floating stiffly out behind her.

"Hello, grandpa," is all she says, for her voice is choked and there are tears in her eyes also.

The old man winks at his grandson and appraises her bountiful beauty with a practiced eye. His ancient finger points first to Michael and then to Denise and then back to Michael again.

"She's with you, Michael, this gorgeous creature?" Nathan Kane asks.

Michael is about to answer and then pauses.

"I think I'll just let her answer that one all by herself!"

Denise nods her head emphatically as her fingers flick a tear from her cheek.

"I'm with him, Grandpa! I am definitely with Michael!"

And suddenly Denise's expression chills. There is the brilliant sun's reflection on the cold steel in her hand. The weapon is there! Michael and Nathan pale and their mouths drop open. Denise springs into a police attack position bracing the gun with one hand while she points it with the other.

Michael is stunned as thoughts propel themselves pell-mell through his mind--Is she the assassin? Is she demonic, possessor of a crazed schizophrenic personality that oscillates without rhyme or reason back and forth between a love goddess and pathological killer? Has the beautiful Denise indeed gone through all this mystery just to execute his grandfather--and him--here on this ocean swept rocky jetty? The questions resonate through his brain without answers in the face of the fearsome gun barrel that menaces them now.

The old man's expression is more one of sheer surprise than fear, the ecstasy of Michael's arrival still fresh with him.

Denise squeezes the trigger twice! BAM! BAM! Nathan and Michael cringe and are frozen in place. The bullets pass by their heads and there is a woman's piercing scream behind them. They turn in time to see her body catapult off the jetty and into the ocean, the clattering of an automatic weapon of some sort ricocheting noisily among the rocks after it flies airborne from her hands. It was the woman who had followed Nathan from the apartment lobby to gather seashells.

A few moments pass before any of the three can speak. Michael has held on to his grandfather throughout the ordeal. He slowly releases him as the realization of what has transpired here begins to dawn on him. He can't help thinking that this Denise is a real piece of work--a truly remarkable woman.

"I'm s-s-sorry," he finally stammers. "For a moment I thought you were aiming that thing at us."

The old man's face breaks out in a broad smile.

"Michael, I'm sure glad you brought this sweet young thing along--and I'm also very glad she's on our side. What did you say her name was?"

"Denise!" Michael shouts.

The impact of what she has done produces a delayed reaction on Denise. She does not speak yet. She glances down at her gun as though she were holding some disgusting viper thing, releasing it quickly from her fingers as though it had contaminated her. Then comes a gush of tears engulfing her lovely body in convulsive sobs. Suddenly she surges at Michael, who was just rising to embrace her. The weight of her on-rushing body pushes him backwards onto the rock and sprawling into the old man. Michael holds on to Denise, tenderly wrapping his muscular arms around her, while Nathan embraces the both of them, tears of happiness streaming down his rugged face.

After a while the tears subside and the three just lie there quietly except for the ocean's roar as it breaks its fury upon the jetty and the occasional screech of a sea gull as it wings by, never having been witness to the strange human configuration that lies there on the rocks beneath it.

Slowly they disengage themselves and assume a sitting position, their legs dangling from the awesome boulder over the spraying ocean. There is no sign of the "hit-man" woman, her body having been carried God knows where by the heaving tide. The sound of gunfire seems to have attracted no attention, as it is not uncommon to hear fisherman shooting at sharks in the area.

Michael is the first to speak when he can.

"Nat," he says, "I'd like you to meet Denise. We met on the plane. Or rather we met the night before. I'm still not sure how or why or who she is, but I do know she saved your life--and I know one other thing for sure: I love her an awful lot."

Tho old man wipes the collected beads

of sweat from his brow.

"Well, Michael," he says, "You sure have said an awful lot in that one mouthful."

Then he addresses himself to the spray-soaked Denise, who has now regained her composure and is smiling.

"Well, young lady. I'm very pleased to make your acquaintance--even under these circumstances. I must admit you had me worried for a moment but I want to thank you for saving my life. I don't think that woman was up to any good."

"No, I don't think so. I'm just glad we could get here in time--and" Denise pauses to take a deep breath, "I can't tell you how long I have looked forward to meeting you, the legendary Nathan Kane."

"Long?" The old man looks puzzled. "How can a child like you know anything about me? Would you like to explain that one to me--plus--and I am most pleased that you are--how do you happen to be here at all? Michael--I was expecting--I almost gave up hope--but he didn't disappoint me--and my son David was a long-shot maybe--but would you care to enlighten this ancient and confused mariner?"

Michael is quick to add his voice to this.

"Denise," he says, "I think it's 'Curtain Up' time also. Thanks for doing what you did, but boy, you sure scared the hell out of me! I really think it's time to explain yourself."

Denise doesn't answer right away but aims her sculptured profile into the sea breeze, her eyes seeming to scan the horizon, looking perhaps for a starting point. Then she turns to face these two Kanes, the young and the old and she can easily visualize the face of the one in between that is missing: David. The faces awaiting her are anxiously attentive and lovingly sympathetic.

"I hate to start this," Denise says, "by saying it's a long story. But it really is. It began rather simply I thought, but I'm afraid it has gotten a little complicated and almost out of hand."

"Go on, go on" the old man urges.

"Some of this is going to really surprise you, grandpa--"

"Please call me Nat--like Michael does."

"O.K. Nat, I hope you won't hate me or think less of me and Michael--you too--you are really going to be shocked--so please prepare yourself. Just remember that everything that happened before I met you really doesn't count. It's too soon to say for sure but I think I love you. Will you please remember that--and try to understand?"

Michael glows a little with the declaration.

"Whatever it is, I forgive you in advance, O.K.?"

Nathan and Michael settle their broad backs against an upright boulder and listen. Denise begins to tell her story, hesitantly haltingly at first and then all the secrets she had held so long just come pouring out.

"My name is Denise Anne Steiner. I was born in New York City where my parents own and operate an international combination private detective and public relations agency. They wanted me to go into the business with them but I had always had a love for the sciences. I wanted to be a scientist, specifically a microbiologist."

She looks away from her wrapt audience for a moment as she senses that the word has hit a resonant cord and there is a small gasp from Michael and a cough from Nathan, as perhaps they both perceive the inkling of things to come.

"I met Dr. David Kane" she continues--.

"DAVID? You mean my son David?" Nathan has to interrupt.

"Yes, Nat, your son David and Michael's father David--the very same.   Anyway I met him when I was his student at
Harvard, a course he gave in molecular
biology.   I was very young and he was
so brilliant and I was just thunderstruck
by him.   He seemed to need someone
desperately--although   I   knew   he   was
married and had a son.   He was so
lonely--but of course he's always been
lonely--alone--isolated.   You know that.
I'm not telling you anything you don't
know."

"Wow," exclaims Michael.   "That is a
shocker!--Go on.   Please go on."

"He seemed to need me.   It wasn't an
emotional thing like love--more like a
psychological and biological need.   And I
was mesmerized by his mind.   We had an
affair.   When the course at Harvard was
over, I followed him to California--where
he had an appointment at Cal Tech.   I
worked with him as a crystallographer--
X-ray photography of cells.   I was good
at it, one of the best.   Despite the relationship, David wouldn't have used me
unless I was the best.   We put everything into it, day and night, scarcely
ever leaving the lab.   It didn't matter.
I worshipped him.   It was what he wanted.   It was what I wanted.   But he
started to feel the strain of guilt as his

wife pressured him for a bigger part in the marriage he was neglecting. He was torn between the two of us. I don't think she knew about me specifically but she knew there was someone."

She takes a deep breath and begins again.

"He offered to leave her and marry me. But I wouldn't let him, and perhaps he didn't mean it. I knew our relationship had to end or it would start affecting his work. In any case, he offered me anything to perpetuate it. I knew it was over. Remember I was young and perhaps foolish. What I wanted was something else, something he didn't want to give. A child. I wanted--I wanted to have something of him forever, something--of us. He was against it on principle, so I'm afraid I tricked him into it. I became pregnant and then I told him it was over. I think he was relieved to get out of it and go back to an uncomplicated life, his work, and his marriage. I never saw him again and he doesn't know that I gave birth to twins, Cindy and Barry."

"Oh my God," says Michael, "you mean those kid's father is my father? Then they are--my half brother and sister!"

"What kids are you talking about?"

Nathan asks.

"Cindy and Barry" says Denise. "They are five years old, Nat. I know how you love children and these are your grandchildren. They are waiting for you back at the lobby."

"Too much," the old man gasps. "This is all too much! Grandchildren, you say? Two yet? A body and a girl, Cindy and Barry? Nice names. My son David's and your children? Now you come and shoot your gun and save my life and say you love Michael here?--You never know what a day will bring when you get up in the morning, do you?"

"How about Kessler, the last name the kids have? Where did that come from? Did you marry?" asks Michael anxiously.

"No. I simply made it up. I couldn't use Kane. I didn't want to use my maiden name Steiner. I wanted it to appear that I was married so I told the hospital the kids' father's name was Kessler."

"Wow!" says Michael lustily. "Well, so far I can live with it. What happened after that? How did you get involved in my life? Coincidence? Or accidently on purpose?"

Denise smiles, and when she does everyone in her presence warms to her radiance. She obviously is feeling better about things at this point.

"On purpose--but I don't want to get ahead of my story. I went home to mother to have the kids and took it easy for about a year. Then I grew restless and started to do some assignments for my father just to keep busy. I grew to like it. It was challenging. I met interesting people. It was exciting. I took training courses including weaponry in police work. I became a marksman-- but I swear to you I have never before fired a gun at a human being--let alone killed anyone.--Do you think we should call the police?"

"The police? Nah!" says Nathan. "They might send their fascist officer Foley. There is no body and so there is no crime. Habeus Corpus, anybody knows that! Go explain what happened here. They'd make a federal case out of it. Forget it! So tell us, how did you happen to get involved with Michael here?"

Denise is now warming to her story.

"Well life went along quite smoothly for me. I had succeeded in forgetting David. The children were doing well. I became more and more involved in my parent's business. Then a few days ago I received an urgent call from my father. He was all excited. Nat's publisher, Steve Richmond, had become very concerned for Nat's life because of the book he was writing and wanted my father to assign an agent to keep an eye on him. When my father heard the name of Nathan Kane, he knew I would have a personal interest in the project. Steve Richmond told me about you, Michael, and arranged for me to meet you at that party through your partner."

"You are quite a little schemer, young lady. And last night, was that part of your scheme?" asks Michael.

"Of course not, silly. I just let nature take its course. I didn't plan to have a meaningful relationship with you. It just happened. I guess I just can't resist the Kane family."

"Listen to this sweet-talk, Nat," Michael says. "I'm listening. I'm listening. So what happened then?" Nat asks.

"Well Michael and I were together and after he got a phone call, he said he had to run. I knew where he was running. Then I got a phone call from Dad saying the situation had grown urgent. People were really trying to kill Nat to keep him from publishing his story. I thought it would be a good time to have my children meet their grandfather so I brought them along. So Nat, what are you going to do now? Are you still going to finish your book?"

Nathan Kane shakes his head vehemently.

"No! No! I confess! It was all a sham, a plot conceived by an old man who didn't want to leave the earth with his son David estranged from him and his son Michael. I arranged the whole thing. I arranged for both David and Michael to learn of my danger and come running to me and make peace with each other. Michael came--but David was too much to ask for. I apologize for meddling and endangering your lives. What can I say after I say I'm sorry."

The response is in unison from Michael and Denise. "We're not sorry! So don't you be!"

The three of them laugh together and put their arms around one another.

Then the old man grows serious for a moment again.

"Denise, darling," he said, "tell me about my son David. The truth now. Don't spare anything. I haven't seen him or spoken to him in a very long time. What did he say when you told him you were leaving him?"

Denise took another deep breath. She had hoped not to go into this but the old man deserved an honest answer.

"He tried to defend himself--he was hurt and he tried to talk me out of it.

Then he tried to explain himself. He began talking about his own father, you, Nat, about what he said was the tremendous waste of all that emotion, the hell between parents and children--I remember his words exactly, 'the ineradicable hell,' he said, and I just shrieked back at him that he had it all wrong, that he had the whole world upside-down, that the only heaven there is is what's between us and our parents and us and our children. He was calm now, that aloof, icy, rational tone of his. He said children and parents were both better off severed from each other as soon as possible, that the Chinese communists had the right idea, that recent studies had shown that... I couldn't stand it, it made me want to retch. I called him a coward, I told him he was afraid of life, that he was pathetic, a freak, and I was about to hang up when he said something I couldn't hear. He coughed nervously, and then I heard him say, "Yes, I agree. But I will tell you a secret--I am what I am because my father is what he is. I didn't choose this for myself. It is because his heart is so large that mine is so small. It was chosen for me, long before I was born, and then he said he had nothing more to say on the subject and he was going to hang up. I said, 'Fine, good, goodbye and good luck!"

The old man sighs a heavy sigh.

"Well, I guess you have answered my question. David isn't going to come. But it was worth it just to see you and Michael together. Now come, give me a hand to get me up off this goddamned rock and let's get out of this miserable sun. I'm a man in a big hurry. I have to go meet my grandchildren. And then I'm going to call Steve Richmond, my publisher, and give him the word. I'll tell him to put out the news that Nathan Kane has retired from being an author and never intended to be a squealer."

Denise and Michael each take an arm and help the old man get to his feet. The two giants and the shapely young woman slowly start to pick their way among the rugged rocks of the jetty away from the precipice overhanging the ocean.

Up ahead on the shore, three teenage girls begin to move slowly away from the shallows and up the beach, their bodies still bent as they scour the dry sand for shells and pieces of coral. Off to the north, the burly man still casts his heavy rod into the surf, although he has been joined by a dog now, the animal racing down to the water each time the tip of the fishing pole arcs swiftly forward.

As they enter the lobby, the threesome are met by a charge of Cindy and Barry, screaming "Mommy, Mommy!" They are introduced to their grandfather who embraces them and hugs them and tousles their hair. There is no recoil or rejection on the part of the children-- only a warm welcome for someone they instinctively know belongs to them. The old man has no need of doctors or pharmaceuticals. He is fairly delirious with joy on the best medicine the world has to offer: the love and nearness of his family.

Michael and Denise hold each other in tight embrace, afraid to let go for fear of having something happen to separate them. They bask in the old man's joy and are happy that the confessions are over.

Back upstairs, Nathan Kane searches the rooms, convinced that Goldmesser must be hiding somewhere, waiting for the right moment to leap out and launch himself into another plea for reason and good sense. And perhaps both Friday and Dr. Henderson lie in wait with the little man, prepared to throw a rope around the old man and haul him off if reason and good sense fail. But the apartment is empty of any sign of them, and Kane notices that even the glasses that were used have been washed and dried and put away, and that the couch has been puffed up and the bed remade.

"Elves," he mutters to himself as he moves through the rooms checking. "Good elves."

"What's that?" Michael calls from the kitchen.

"Nothing," Nathan answers. "Just wondering where everyone has gotten to. Ah, here's a note. It's from Friday. Let's hear what he has to say.

"Dear Mr. Kane:

The doorman Joe told us that you were in good hands, that Michael and a lady friend had gone out to be with you. Parthenia (Dr. Henderson) and I find that we have an awful lot to talk about so we are going out for a while. Mr. Goldmesser went down to his apartment to call the phone company to get your phone fixed. See you later.

Friday"

The children drag Denise out on the patio from which they can see out for miles to where the ocean meets the sky.

The two men are left alone for a moment.

"Well what do you think of her, Nat?

I know when it comes to women you are
a <u>mavin</u>."

"She is a gem, Michael, a jewel among
jewels. Don't let her get away--although
it doesn't look like you could if you
wanted to, you lucky stiff."

The old man playfully slaps the
younger man's cheek.

"There is one thing that is a little
squeamish for me though, Nat. I hope
it won't prove to be a problem."

They sit down together face to face
across the coffee table.

"The kids," Michael says. "It's a
little strange raising your father's kids
as your own and living with a woman as
your wife that has borne your father's
kids."

"That's all in the past, Michael.
Don't dwell on it or you will sour up a
perfectly sweet situation. Now is now!
And what has been is long since over.
Get your divorce and marry this girl as
soon as you can! And those kids are
Kane's or Kapulkins or whatever--but
they are great!"

They laugh together, a rich, wonderful sound, full of life and a certain
acknowledgement of its ironies, and
Michael reaches across the table and
grips Nathan's shoulder.

"I love you, old man," Michael Kane

says.

Kane nods, his eyes fastened on the eyes of his grandson, eyes that could be his own.

"Let's get those kids and Denise something to eat, they must be hungry. So, kiddo, you got any appetite after all you've been through? You want to feed your face a little?" Kane pushes away from the table and stands up. "I still only have one regret out of all this."

"What is that?" Michael says.

"It's too bad your father didn't come to see me also," the old man says.

Morning, the following day

The day dawns with an angry snarl, the sun rising with blistering rage. It is not yet seven, yet already the city bakes. Out toward the beach, where the hotels and condominiums squat shoulder to shoulder mile after mile, it is Sunday and nothing stirs save the occasional Saturday-night reveler sneaking wearily homeward and here and there groups of security and maintenance men changing shifts. North, where the more expensive dwellings stretch out at more leisurely intervals, Harbor House stands roasting under the sun's merciless shower of flame. You look and you think the interior must be a furnace, yet within

the air is cool. Even here, high up on
the topmost floor, a chill current of air
cuts through the quiet rooms, pushed by
the powerful machinery roaring in the
vast sub-cellar below.

Everything up here is white, so white
that it is like stepping inside a refrigerator, an effect that is heightened by
the smooth contours that confront the
eye where ever you turn. Come into the
bedroom, then, where the huge figure
modelled against the stark sheets moves.
He rolls to his side, takes a deep
breath, and then cants his feet to the
floor below. Again he breathes deeply,
fingers his hands back through his mass
of blazing hair, and with a groan of
effort, stands. The body, naked, is
enormous, its musculature, though ra-
vaged, still evident, the skin the color
of oak that has been lightly stained and
then finished with a coat of something
that makes it gleam.

Nathan Kane moves across the white
carpet into the dressing room and then,
beyond it, into the large bathroom aglow
in the burnished rays refracted by the
skylight overhead. With his hands on
his hips and his shoulders thrown back,
the old man stands before the toilet and
urinates, the stream driving long and
hard into the water below.

"Still like an ox," he says aloud, and then sighs.

He reaches down, pressing the lever, and then turns to the large white marble sink behind him, running water and splashing it over his face and under his arms. With his hands still wet, he runs his fingertips through his hair, combing the wild mane back so that tails of white show against the creased, bronze leather at the back of his neck.

He feels his cheeks, the coarse white bristles sounding as he rubs upward, and then he checks his beard in the mirror and decides against it. Even the fast brushing he gives his teeth seems to him a nuisance in the light of the urgency he feels to be in motion, to begin the proving the day demands.

He does not bother to dry his face. He steps into the dressing room and selects a clean pair of trousers and a long-sleeved shirt, both white, both cotton, both identical to the shirt and trousers he wore the day before.

He folds back the sleeves to just above his elbows, and he spreads the collar as far as it will go. Satisfied, he seats himself in the white canvas camp chair, and pulls into his tennis shoes, wheezing and coughing as he bends to tie double knots.

Kane stands and returns to the side of the bed. He reaches down to the small night-table and takes up his wrist-watch and straps it on. Then he gathers up the wallet and the coins and the ring of keys that are also lying there. He straightens and squares his shoulders, and then he goes from the master bedroom into the living room.

It is brighter in here, and the room is accordingly not so cold. Yet the old man moves first to the couch, to lift the sheet higher and thus to cover the sleeping man's shoulders. The couch is king-size yet it seems to be suffering under the great piling weight. Nathan Kane listens for a moment, to hear the even breathing of slumber, and then he crouches lower, close to the thick blonde hair, and he touches this hair with his lips, his lips parted and murmuring "I'm glad you came."

The apartment is a lush three bedroom affair that has entrances on the foyer leading away from the living room. One of the other bedrooms belongs to Friday. The old man pauses at his closed door, smiles and shakes his head.

"You rascal, you," he whispers softly. "Dr. Parthenia Henderson really got to you, eh?"

Friday had returned late, very

embarrassed at his absence yet his eyes glowing with a radiance Nathan Kane had never seen in him before. The old man reveled in Friday's happy enamored state. That Dr. Henderson was a rara avis--something special--but with the personalities as they were, Nathan Kane thought they would need a permanent referee.

The old man moves on and pauses at the last bedroom door. It is slightly ajar and he can see the outlines of the bodies in the two double bed arrangement. In one he sees the two children sleeping curled against each other atop the white quilt that has been intended as a coverlet, their caps of soft flowing hair like two distant trekkers frozen in fearful embrace on a field of infinite snow.

A second quilt lies twisted at their ankles, and the old man groans with the effort as he kneels to raise it and smooth it over the small huddling bodies. When the old man reaches to wedge the coverlet in snugly around them, he feels their breathing against his hand, and for a time he lets that large hand rest there, lightly, his eyes closed, his features softened by his reverie.

Nathan Kane wakens from his pensiveness and glances over at the other bed. He feels a blush of embarrassment as though he has intruded into a nymph's private boudoir, for even in sleep Denise is a vision of poetic beauty. Her exquisite face is pillowed in her cascading hair, one soft outstretched arm and shoulder exposed beyond her cover as though she were reaching for something. The trace of a soft smile trails from her sensuous lips and Nathan Kane feels surely she is experiencing a pleasurable dream.

The old man contemplates this re-markable woman and can't help thinking how fate has so fortunately continued to bizarrely entwine this lovely stranger's life with his own. David--and the chil-dren--then Michael--then saving him from the female assassin out on the jetty. He silently throws Denise a kiss and quietly moves out of the bedroom, through the foyer and back into the liv-ing room. He enters the kitchen think-ing to make himself a cup of instant coffee to tide himself over til he can have a real Sunday breakfast with the whole gang. The clock on the wall shows it's just seven o'clock--too early yet to call down for a delivery of lox and bagels and cream cheese and her-ring--the kind of stuff he thinks that Jewish breakfasts are made of.

Suddenly he is alerted to a gentle tapping at the door. Goldmesser--no doubt--probably forgot his glasses here somewhere and considerate enough not to ring the doorbell and waken everyone. On second thought Nathan Kane grows cautious--perhaps still another assassin sent to avenge the others. He remembers that he forgot to call his publisher Steve Richmond to tell him to publicize the fact Nathan Kane will not write his book.

The old man tiptoes to the door and stealthily takes a peek through the peephole. His heart nearly stops as he squints hard to get a better look. Can it be? Is it possible? David? Here and now? It certainly looks like him though his hair is already speckled with gray. There are evident aging lines creeping into the handsome face which is darkened somewhat by a beard stubble that has not been shaved this morning.

Nathan Kane's hand trembles as he fumbles to unlock and open the door and they face each other--at long last-- father and son. No audible words are heard as both their lips move to try to find and form the right thing to say. How does one greet a prodigal son or for that matter a prodigal father? The old man listens fearfully to the silence until

it leaps into thunder with a single word:
"Dad?"

"Yes," the old man says, and now he wonders if he will be capable of anything more.

Nathan Kane wants to sit down or fall down or lie down. He wants to get very close to the earth and burrow in. He wants to get under something, inside something, to be where it's dark and empty and nobody else is. But the old man stands there, struggling to keep to his feet and to stand very straight, his pale eyes watering slightly, his body stiff with the will to be ready for whatever will come next.

"I'm here," the old man says. "It's me."

"Yes, it is you," David Kane says, "You see I came." There is a brief silence again.

The old man manages a weak smile.

"I'm very glad that you did."

"It's been a long time," David says. "Years, I suppose. I suppose I should have called when Mother died. I suppose I should have called then--or flown in--beforehand. Or for the funeral. I suppose I should have--said something, done something. But what difference would it have made? You know how I am. There's no sense hiding it or faking it."

"I know," the old man says. "All that matters is that you are here now."

"You know why I came, don't you? On the plane flying in from L.A. I figured it out," says David.

"Believe it or not, David, I was sure that you would. You were always a smart boy," the old man says and they are both a little embarrassed by his last remark.

"I made a discovery that was as important as any I have ever made in a laboratory," David says. "Firstly, what most people know instinctively from birth, others--if they are lucky--discover in an Edisonian eureka fashion."

"What was that?" Nathan Kane asks.

"That no man is an island! Fundamental, isn't it? Yet so difficult to learn for someone who has felt isolated for so long. And do you know what triggered it, Dad?" David asks. "Because maybe there is also a lesson here for both of us."

"God knows I'm not too old to learn. What is it?"

"Simply that sometimes it is more important to be needed than to be loved. I couldn't handle all your love but I got the message when I thought you needed me."

Nathan Kane extends his hand cautiously across the entrance threshhold and his son takes the gnarled fingers in his own and squeezed them firmly. The contract of skin on skin seems to dissolve the wall of resistance that has stood between them for so many years. The dam collapses before the surge of emotional feeling and they are swept into each other's arms. For the first time that either can remember, David Kane cries like a baby and his father sobs with him, cradling him and gently patting his back.

A passerby would surely have wondered and marveled at this heart-rending sight--two giant men holding each other and sobbing in an open doorway at seven o'clock on a Sunday morning in the penthouse apartment. But there were no passerbys--no eyes to see, no ears to hear.

The old man was the first to speak.

"Look at us, standing in the doorway like a couple of fools. Come on in, David. I was just going to make some coffee."

David nervously dabs a handkerchief to his eyes and glances into the apartment.

"Is anyone else here. I'm not very presentable didn't even stop to shave--

rushed right over."

"Well, as a matter of fact," Nathan Kane says, "there are some people here that you know very well and others that you ought to know better."

"Michael?" David asks, "I knew Michael would be here. I'd very much like to see him--but not yet--I'd like to clean up first. Who else?"

Nathan Kane raises both arms as if asking heavenly guidance.

"Who else, you ask? Better prepare yourself for a big shocker because this I'm sure you did not expect, no matter how smart you are. Tell you what, David. Come on down to the pool area. You can shave and shower and we can talk. O.K.?"

The pool area is deserted at this early hour. David has refreshed himself and father and son settle down on deck chairs across an umbrella-shaded table. The talk starts slowly, hesitatingly, both men feeling their way, finding it impossible to breach a lifetime of difference in one fell swoop. They quickly mutually agree to forget the past and attend to the present. David is now able to speak calmly, unemotionally, feeling a blazing exhileration in the fact that he could express himself so freely.

"I came because I knew you were

sending for me, asking for me. I felt
an irresistible need to go to you that I
could no more ignore than pretend that I
did not have to breathe. I guess there
is an eternal life-line between fathers
and sons that cannot be torn or lost for-
ever--and shouldn't be. I have been a
fool. I lost a father and a son for too
long and I really came to reclaim them."

The old man listens patiently, his
ears hearing the words he has longed to
hear--dispaired of ever hearing, and
now rejuvenating him with their sound.

"Tell me, David, did you really believe that my life was in danger? Is
that why you decided to come original-
ly?"

"At first, yes," David says. "But
then as I said I figured it out. I instinctively knew that you were calling
for me."

"To tell you the truth, David, I got
more action out of this book business
than I bargained for," the old man says.
"I was shot at, almost bombed, and almost shot at again--which brings me to
who else is up in the apartment."

Nathan Kane tells David about Denise
and her children--his children--and poor
David is shocked and confused. And
then the old man explains all the circumstances and coincidences with Michael

and that no one bears David any ill will or has any demands on him. Michael and Denise are very much in love and plan to marry--as soon as Michael gets his divorce--and raise the children as their own--unless of course David has some objection.

"No! No! Of course not," he says. He rises to his feet and looks out over the pool area out towards the ocean. He seems deep in thought for a moment and Nathan sits quietly knowing there is a great deal of mental adjustment his son is struggling to make.

"Dad," David finally says, "have you called your publisher yet to tell him that you were not going to finish the book? You know, so the word will get out and they'll call of their dogs?"

Nathan jumps to his feet.

"I'm glad you reminded me," he says. I meant to do that this morning."

"Well, wait up," David says. "I have sort of a proposition for you."

The old man seems genuinely surprised.

"A proposition? What is it, David?"

David paces a bit before he speaks.

"Now, please Dad. Don't feel that you are obligated to do this--and if you don't think it's a good idea--I know you'll just say so right out, won't you?"

"Sure, David, sure. You know me. What is it?"

"This book," David says, "that you were going to write. I would like to do it with you--you know--collaborate on it--only one important thing--fictionalize it--you know--any resemblance to persons living or dead purely coincidental. That way nobody can get mad. What do you say? Want to think about it?"

Nathan Kane slaps his hands together and dances a little jig.

"I don't have to think about it! That's a great idea! We'll work together on it! Can you spare the time, though, David--from your important work?"

"I'll take a leave of absence. I need it," David says happily.

"Come on David. Let's go tell the others: Michael, Denise and the kids. I want to tell my friends Friday and Goldmesser too," Nathan Kane says as he wraps his arm around David's shoulders and they head back for the apartment.

"I've got an awful lot to tell them," David says. "I especially want them to know about "Our Fathers Before Us.""